BEYOND THE WINDOW

DIANE WINTERS

Copyright © 2020 SECOND EDITION BY DIANE WINTERS

ISBN: 9798652708764

All rights reserved

The characters and events portrayed in this book are fictitious. Any similarity to real persons, living or dead, is coincidental and not intended by the author.

No part of this book may be reproduced, stored in a retrieval system, or transmitted in any form or by any means, electronic, mechanical, photocopying, recording, or otherwise, without express written permission of the publisher.

Printed in the United States of America

PART ONE

Edna Chessmore stood in front of the bedroom window, looking out at the unkempt yard. If anyone could see her, they would be surprised by the matted gray, curly hair and ratty, old bathrobe. It was three in the afternoon, and Edna looked like she had just gotten up after a long week in a sickbed. They wouldn't be far from wrong. She had been holed up in her bedroom for months, caring little how she looked to anyone, including herself.

Her view was the backyard surrounded by a small forest of trees. It offered a cool canopy in the summer and provided protection from the snow in the winter. The property was immense. The fence line around it delineated it from the neighbors more than it was used to keep people out. She turned and looked toward her favorite rose garden and realized it had grown wild and spread into areas that were supposed to be kept for the cook's garden.

As she finished her tea, Edna heard her maid come in behind her. "What is it, Martha?"

Martha came over and handed Edna a business card. Mr. Harrison has arrived. He says you asked him to come."

Edna looked at the card. "Thank you, Martha. Please tell him he'll have to wait since he didn't call ahead of time. I need to clean up." Martha nodded and left the room.

Edna sighed, looked out the window one more time, then headed for her on-suite bathroom. A half-hour later, she was trying to decide what to wear when Martha returned.

"Yes, Martha?"

"Mr. Harrison says he's sorry he didn't call first, and he is happy to wait for you. Can I help you, ma'am?"

Edna continued to look at her closet. "I hate all of these clothes. Help me find something."

Martha went to the bureau, pulled out a soft sweater, and picked out some slacks. "Ma'am, just dress casually. The gentleman is not wearing a suit."

"Thank you, Martha. I haven't had clothes on for so long, I couldn't decide. These will be just fine. Please tell Mr. Harrison I will be down shortly. Oh, wait. Please take the robe and gown in the bathroom and burn them."

Martha left with the worn-out clothes in tow, and Edna finally managed to get dressed and her hair brushed out. The natural curls bounced as she attempted to get them under control. *"Forget it."* She tied her hair back and threw the brush on the dressing table. Edna left her bedroom for the first time in months. She was surprised that nothing had changed as she walked to the den, although she didn't know why. Her life was tipped upside down, so she assumed everything else was, too. She opened the door to the den and glided in to see her guest, and reached out her hands to take his, but he gave her a huge hug instead.

"Max, how have you been?"

"The question is, how are you doing? I've tried to see or call you for weeks."

"I'm still here."

Max looked at Edna and then led her to the big, overstuffed wingback chairs by the window. "It's been a long time since we've talked, but you wouldn't have called me to come unless there is something you need. What can I do for you? Whatever you need, I'm your man."

Edna sat looking at her hands and noticed the veins started to show more. Her clothes were too big, and her rings, as she fidgeted with them, were loose enough to fall off on their own. When she finally looked up at Max, she noticed he was sitting there patiently, waiting for her to gather her thoughts. He was so quiet that she almost forgot he was there.

"It's been a long six months. I stopped leaving my room, taking calls, or reading my mail. This is the first day I dressed for weeks, and Martha needed to help me pick out my clothes. Max, I have to get myself back into my old life. It's stupid for me to waste away and be on the pity pot. I might be old, but I'm not old enough to continue my current trajectory. I stood looking out my window, and everything I cared so much about was gone or a mess. I was shocked to see my rose garden looking as frazzled as I feel." She paused.

Max leaned forward and took Edna's hands in his. "You have so many friends, and you've shut them all out. Let me help you get back out in public. You can't do it by yourself and I assumed you would want my help, but I don't know why you waited so long."

"Because I was completely nonfunctioning. I'm just now waking up, and I don't like what I see."

Max sat back. "Did George leave you in good financial shape?"

Edna sighed. "Yes."

"So, I don't need to help you?"

"No, Max. I have my people paying the bills, so I didn't get behind."

"Okay. That's a relief. Where do you want to go first?"

"The office. It's past time I go back, and I need to feel alive again."

"How about I take you out for supper afterward?"

"As long as it's a quiet place. My first day back is going to be pretty stressful."

"You got it." Max stood up and reached for her hands. He pulled her up and gave her another hug. "Don't you think you should consider selling out and retiring? I know that place is your baby, but seriously. I worry about you and all of the sharks circling the waters."

Edna laughed. "When I get back, I'll see how I feel. Evidently, they've been doing fine without me all this time. They're probably glad I've been gone. You know, while the cat's away?"

"I'll pick you up in the morning, and then at 5:00 p.m. sharp, I will get you out of there. If you need me before then, just give me a call."

"Thanks, Max. I knew I could count on you to throw me back out to the wolves."

The following day, Edna managed not only to pick out her own clothes, but she went to the kitchen for a cup of coffee and her breakfast. The cook was astonished to see her but recovered quickly.

"It's good to see you, ma'am. Wouldn't you like breakfast in the dining room?"

"No, Sarah. The kitchen is fine, thank you. From now on, I'm eating in here. I won't be home for supper this evening, either."

"Yes, ma'am. I'll see you in the morning then."

Edna watched for Max and walked out to the car as he drove up. Max drove a dark-blue BMW with soft golden-colored leather seats, and the car glided through traffic without difficulty. The two spoke little because she was so nervous.

He pulled up in front of her office and said, "Go get em,' Tiger."

Edna smiled and got out of the car. With one last look at Max, she threw back her shoulders and opened the door to her building.

"Mrs. Chessmore. It's good to see you again." The building receptionist was so loud, it took her back for a moment.
"Yes, dear. It's good to see you too."

She headed for the elevators and waited for the doors to open. She began to feel the pressure building inside her and started to have a panicky feeling. The doors mercifully opened, and there was no one else in the car. She quickly hit the close button and waited a moment to push the button for her floor. She took some deep breaths and attempted to calm herself before finally hitting the right button.

Edna barely got herself under control when the doors opened, and everyone from her office was standing there clapping their hands as she came off of the elevator. She forced a smile and thought about killing the downstairs receptionist. Edna tried to talk to everyone in turn and hoped she could go hide in her office. She finally spotted her own secretary and grabbed her by the arm. Doris felt her anxiety and helped Edna get into her office and shut the door.

"Thank you for rescuing me, Doris. That was very nice but way too much stimulation for my first day back."

Edna took a few deep breaths and walked to the window. It was a view she had always loved. At night, you could see the lights of the city and the traffic patterns. During the day, she always enjoyed the different sights. As much as she loved the outdoors, she didn't know why she always managed to work inside. Doris let her stand there and relax and watched her shoulders loosen up before interrupting her.

"It's good to have you back. You are back, aren't you?"

"I don't know. I think so. I guess we'll see how this goes." She turned and smiled at Doris, pointed to a chair, and sat at her own desk. "Tell me what I've missed. Do I still have the same staff doing the same jobs? What problems have there been?"

Doris spent the next two hours catching her up on what had been happening in the office. Edna began to become agitated and stopped Doris.

"Let me catch my breath. I can't believe I've missed out on so much."

Doris went to her own office and made them both some tea, which gave Edna time to relax. She stood up and went back to her window again until Doris returned. She asked her about her family and about the health of her employees. Her secretary was definitely part of the gossip mill. They enjoyed their tea before getting back to business.

Chessmore Industries had multiple entities, but they were all interrelated. The company was well known for its top-of-the-line care and products. First of all, she owned a dozen retirement centers in a tri-state area. Then as a side business, she owned a laundry company that handled not only her own retirement centers but contracted with other nursing and retirement homes in the area to provide crisp and clean products. Their contracts never had to worry about torn or stained products. She also created a commercial cleaning business that provided staff not only to her own centers but contracted to any other type of business needing assistance. Edna made sure her employees were paid well, and many people had been with her companies for several years. Some of her current managers worked their way up to their positions, and she was proud of their accomplishments to help grow the company.

Her husband, George, was a corporate lawyer and wrote up the contracts for her. But Edna had always been the face of her own business. Although she was financially stable in her own right, George's job was the breadwinner. The long hours finally took a toll on him, and he died of a massive heart attack one evening while out with friends. One of those friends was Maximilian Harrison.

Edna was glad to see the end of the day arrive. She spent most of the day catching up on long-overdue communication and apologizing to companies that had all but given up on her calling them back. Exhaustion set in as her day came to a close. She and Doris took the elevator down together, and Edna found Max waiting for her out front. She jumped into the car and leaned back into the soft seat, letting out a big sigh as he pulled out into traffic.

"Tough day?"
"Terribly so. I'm ready for a large glass of wine before we eat."
"You got it."

Max sped down the street and turned into the parking lot of a quaint Italian restaurant. It was early for the supper crowd, and they were led directly to a table in a corner that looked out on the street. They ordered their drinks, and Edna sat back to relax. She looked out the window for a while, watching the rush hour traffic. Her wine was delivered, and she took an unusually large drink.

"This is good wine."
"It must be because you downed half a glass."
Edna looked down at the glass and chuckled. "I hope tomorrow is easier, but I'm so far behind."
"You'll be fine. It will take a while to get caught up to speed, but you'll get there. Want me to pick you up tomorrow?"
"No. I'll start getting myself to work. I need to pull on my big girl panties and just do it. I do appreciate the offer, though, and I so appreciated you getting me to work and back today. I even had a hard time getting on the elevator and up to my office, so just getting me to the office was an accomplishment on its own."

Edna began to relax, and Max made her first evening out a pleasure. He regaled her with stories of parties he had gone to and how people always asked about her. Many of their mutual friends sent her invitations, but she refused to even look at the mail. She suddenly felt guilty about ignoring everyone.

"Max, I'll try to get a hold of them soon. Maybe I'll even hold my own get-together."
"Now, that sounds like our friend Edna."

Max took her home after their relaxing evening, which included a bottle of wine that Edna mostly consumed by herself. Before letting her get out of the car, he reached for her hand.

"Edna, you and George were always there for me. When I lost Jane, I was bereft. Just remember I'll be here for you whenever you need me."
"I appreciate it, Max. I knew you were what I needed to get out of the house again. It made my day go a lot easier knowing you'd be there for me at the end of the day."

He patted her hand, and Edna got out, waved goodbye, and went into her own sanctuary. The week progressed in a flurry of paperwork. The more Edna got done, the more Doris brought in to her. More than once, she kicked herself for letting things go so long without her oversight. By Friday afternoon, she wondered if she would ever catch up. Then Doris came into her office empty-handed.

"What? No bundle of reports?" she said, smiling.

"Actually, no. We are at the bottom of the report barrel. Next week we can start on the financial reports. That shouldn't take too long since your CPAs have continued to handle all of that. If you want, I'll run the reports off, and you can take them home over the weekend."

"I might as well since I don't have any other commitments, I'd just wonder what they looked like, and probably fret all weekend anyway."

"I'll be right back. I'll have them printed off before you gather your things to leave."

Edna looked around. She was surprised at how much work she had accomplished and happy she found only a few surprises in the mix. Her team had done a nice job without her. She grabbed her purse and a few papers she wanted to review and stuffed them in her bag.

Doris, true to her word, was back with a large accordion folder filled with papers. "I have each business in its own folder. The corporate papers are in the front."

"How does it look?"

"I don't know. You know that I don't deal with the financials. I don't even balance my own checkbook."

"For such an excellent secretary, I believe that's your only flaw. What am I to do with you?" They both laughed, and Edna headed for the elevators. "See you Monday. Have a great weekend."

"So glad you're back, Mrs. Chessmore. We've really missed you." Edna gave a small wave as the elevator doors closed on a successful week.

The evening was cool enough to sit on the patio for her meal, so Edna decided to change into some old jeans and a T-shirt and enjoy herself. She got so used to lounging around that her work attire was stifling. After her supper, she wandered around the backyard, looking directly at her rose garden and yard. *"This will never do."*

There was plenty of daylight left, so she went to the garden shed for her clippers and gloves. By the time dusk arrived, Edna had a large pile of trimmings, and her rosebushes were tamed and brought back to order. She vowed to work in the yard over the weekend.

While Edna fussed in the rose garden, the staff watched from inside. They commented on the sudden change in her behavior from being cooped up in her room to working every day. They were glad to see her back to a normal routine, but now they were worried she was doing too much too soon. The staff loved the Chessmores and were always been treated with respect. It was almost as devastating to the staff as it was to Edna when George suddenly passed away.

Edna looked at the rose garden one more time before going back into the house. She was bone tired and decided a hot shower, and retiring early for the night was next on her schedule. Once out of the shower, she looked around her bedroom suite. Having stayed in the same room for the past six months, somehow it looked different. Then she realized that the drapes were open, the bed was freshly made, and the room smelled clean.

"I was a slug." Edna crawled between her sheets and picked up a book lying on her nightstand that she had no

recollection of choosing. Opening the cover, she didn't think she had ever started this particular book. She turned to the first chapter and only got to the second page before falling asleep, dropping the book to the floor. Martha walked by later to check on her and peeked in. She came into the room, picked the book up off the floor, shut off the light, and closed the door softly.

The weekend stretched out before Edna like the Grand Canyon. She had so much time with so little to do. "Martha, will you call our old gardener and see if I can retain his services again? I feel like I got hit by a truck after spending all that time in the rose garden."
"Yes, ma'am. I'll get right on that and let you know. If he doesn't have the time, I know someone else that might take the job."
"Very good, Martha. I'll leave you to the decision then. As much as I love to spend the time outdoors, I think it's too far gone for me to manage."

After asking Sarah to bring her in some tea later, Edna strode to the den and sat at her desk. She pulled the accordion file out of the bag and sorted the financials into piles on her desk. Starting with the corporate file, she attempted to read through the numbers. Her mind felt muddled, and her eyes blurred. She got up and headed toward her favorite spot by the window. *"Maybe I've lost my edge."* She continued staring out the window but didn't really focus on any one thing. Sarah brought the tea tray in, set it down beside Edna, and poured her a cup of hot tea.

"Thank you, Sarah. Fix yourself a cup."

Sarah nodded and rushed off to get her own cup. When she returned, Edna pointed to the extra chair across from her. They sat in a comfortable silence for a few minutes, watching the birds in the yard finding bugs and seeds.

"Sarah, I feel like I'm adrift on a raft at sea. I spent all week catching up, but now that I have a day off, I don't have the desire to do anything. The spark seems to be gone. Maybe Max is right, and I should sell out and retire."

Sarah sat quietly and listened. She wasn't sure if she was expected to say anything or give advice, so she continued to sip her tea. Edna continued to look out the window and seemingly was in another world.

"I miss George so much."
"Martha and I do, too, Mrs. Chessmore."
"I know, dear. Thank you for saying that. You know, all in all, we had a good marriage. I haven't felt this listless since we lost our son. Then George and I spent the next several years working so we didn't have to think about his loss." She paused. "As you know, our son was named Xavier. George thought he should have a regal and tough name. I accepted it, but I never did like it. He grew into his name, though. Xavier was a warrior in the Marines. He spent six years doing who knows what. All I knew was that it was dangerous. When he got out, he spent the next four years in Washington, DC, working for the government, and then suddenly he was gone. He's been gone almost six years now, and here I sit in this huge house and stare out the windows." She turned to Sarah. "This is no way to live, and I appreciate you sticking with me these last few months."

"We were really worried about you. There is no way

we could leave you in your condition."

Edna looked at her questioningly. "Now that I snapped out of it, are you thinking of leaving?"

"No, ma'am. That's not what I meant. I just mean that we consider you our own family, and we take care of family, not leave when things go south."

"Thank you, Sarah. I appreciate everything you and Martha have done for me. They would have locked me up a long time ago if it hadn't been for you two caring souls."

They sat for a while over the second cup of tea before Sarah excused herself. Edna took a deep breath and went back to the desk. She reviewed the financials she previously looked at, and then set them aside. Pulling another set toward her, she diligently went through every line.

As she finished the last of the financials, she began to frown. Something wasn't quite right, but she couldn't put her finger on it. She took a break, stretched, and started over. Separately, the pages looked all right, but when she looked at them in a total overview, she was concerned. Edna put everything in the folder and tucked it away. The first thing on her agenda for Monday morning was to contact her accountants.

******

Edna wouldn't be able to see Carson Shoemaker to discuss her financials until later in the day. She spent most of the morning looking and comparing previous financials and still couldn't figure out the discrepancy. Something was amiss, and she wanted answers.

She left for lunch and walked downtown for a sandwich at one of her favorite haunts. It was a mom-and-pop café and was not frequented by the younger generation as much as the trendy ones across the street. She was welcomed like a lost friend and visited for several minutes with the owners before going to her favorite table. It wasn't long before her piping hot homemade soup and sandwich were brought to her. The cheese melting between the crusts made her regret having waited so long between visits.

Enjoying the walk back to the office, she was unaware of being followed. She turned into her building and went on up to her office where she remained until it was time for her to leave for the accountants. Doris had several items for her to attend to, and it made time fly.

Edna left the office for the day and wished everyone a good evening before entering the elevator. She got out on the garage level and found her keys as she went to her car. She got in and shut the door and automatically locked them. Just as she was turning the key, she heard a tap on her side window, which made her jump.

"Got any money?" The man was dressed in filthy clothes and was standing there, leering at her through the window.
"I never carry cash. Sorry."

Edna started the car and moved slowly away from the man. She mentioned to the garage attendant that someone was in the garage begging, and he promised her he would look into it. She arrived at her appointment with the accountant a little early and took the time to look around the building. Chessmore Industries used this accountant since its inception, and George had been a good friend of the founder. The office was modestly furnished, and the building was an updated colonial house. The entryway was refurbished using the old staircase, burnished oak in color. The offices were all on the main floor, and the upstairs was used for storage of records and nonpublic uses.

The kitchen was still used as a break room, and everyone was allowed free reign to cook a meal for lunch. It also came in handy for luncheon meetings when the staff needed to get together. The waiting room was the old parlor, and it still had a working fireplace. The living room was the owner's office and was also used for meetings due to its size. The partners each had their own office, and somewhere tucked away, they each had a secretary answering the phone and assisting their boss.

The bell on the door announced a client's arrival, and someone would mysteriously arrive to show them to the parlor. Edna always loved the allure and ambiance of the office and how it was set up. Compared to her sterile, stressful, businesslike setting downtown, this was very peaceful and quiet.

Carson Shoemaker arrived to take Edna to his office. Her copies of the financials had scribbled red markings all over. They got right to work, and Carson became more confused as he reviewed the paperwork.

"Just a minute. None of this makes any sense, and no one has brought it to my attention before." He pulled up her files on his computer and hit Print. He laid his copy beside hers. "We have a problem. These are my original numbers. Yours have been altered." He pointed to her paperwork.

"Here, here, and here."

Edna stared at the information and then looked at Carson. "What's going on?"

"I don't know, but someone is manipulating your figures to their advantage. You're lucky, though. It's only been since you've been off."

"What do I do now?"

Leaning back in his chair, Carson thought about the problem. "Don't tell anyone you suspect problems. Just watch and wait. Someone will eventually tip their hands. I assume it's an amateur because it's poorly done. You would have caught this right away if you had been in the office. They may have been taking a few bucks here and there, and when you were gone, they decided to be brave and delve into your pocketbook. We find that embezzlers usually have a gambling problem or other debt issues, and it's also just poor money management on their part. You should probably check to see who has access to your checking account and the financial files. When people have been in business as long as you have, staff come and go, and before you know it, computer security gets lax. Call your IT man and have him work on cleaning up the systems. You will need to have him do all of the offices, not just yours."

Edna was taking notes and nodded as Carson talked. "Once you have your security tightened up, someone may come up to you and ask why they can't get into a certain file or have access to something. That will be your first clue. Investigate their position and have them explain why they need access. It could be a legitimate reason, but you hope that the guilty party is found that way. You also need to check out the staff that does the accounts payable and receivables. And who has access to your bank account? Those types of things. Have the IT guy check your server for a hacker. Start with your office and work your way out. While he is doing that, rerun a background check on all of your employees, including the IT people. I'll keep a closer eye on things here to see if I can tell where I could be getting bogus information from. I'll have our IT guy check our server, too."

"Oh, Carson. Good Lord. What a mess. Why didn't I come back to work sooner?"

"Whoever is doing this is sneaky. With you out of the picture, they got brave. You might consider one more option."

"What's that?"

"A private investigator. Have your employees checked for a sudden change in their lifestyle or financial status."

"That does make sense—quiet, unobtrusive, and no one would know. I can pay for that personally so it doesn't show up on the books anywhere. I wonder . . ." She paused.

"Yes?"

"Maybe I better have you check George's financials too. It could be someone from his old office, and they could have gotten access to my records somehow."

"That's a good idea. Let me check into that too."

They discussed more options before Edna left for home, mulling over the suggestions by Carson. He gave her the number of a private investigator to call, and she promised to get right on it. Preoccupied with her thoughts, she didn't realize she was being followed again.

Once she was settled in her den after supper, she reached over to make a call and changed her mind. Fishing around in her purse, she located her cell phone, which hadn't been charged for weeks. Edna finally found the charger and plugged it in. While waiting, she took a stroll in the garden area. The roses were all setting on, and it smelled glorious. Looking at the yard, she noticed a gardener had come by, and it changed the appearance of her whole yard. She walked around the yard and caught movement out of the corner of her eye. She turned to look but couldn't see anything or anyone. A chill went up her spine, so she rushed back into the house and locked the patio door. Closing the curtains, she walked toward the kitchen.

"Sarah? Have you seen any strangers around here lately?"

"Strangers? No, ma'am. Where?"

"In the yard. Are we still locking everything up tight at night?"

"Yes, ma'am, before we head to bed we check all the doors."

"Make sure you do. I could swear someone was in the yard just now."

"Oh, my. I hope not. I'll make sure the floodlights are switched on, too. It will alert us if someone is out there."

"Thank you. I must be paranoid, but it certainly made me skittish."

She went back to the den but left her door open. She turned on the CD player and inserted some soft, calming music then looked at her cell phone. There was enough power to use it again, so she sat down and got out the business card Carson gave her.

After several rings, she heard someone pick up and say gruffly, "Jordan here."
"Yes, this is Edna Chessmore. I'd like to meet you somewhere about a job. I have a huge project for you to consider if you have the time."
"Are you going to give me a clue?"
"I don't want to discuss this over the phone."
"Gotcha. Meet me at Jindels at three on Wednesday. Do you know where that is?"
"I believe so. How will I know you?"
"Find a booth. I'll find you. Can you take a selfie and send it to me?"
"It's been a while, but I think so."
"See you on Wednesday. Come early and wait for me. I'll let you know then if I'll take the job."
"Thank you."

Jordan hung up the phone before her sentence was completed. *"Rude man."* After messing with her phone, she remembered how to take her own picture and sent it to the number.

The following day, she called in the IT tech, Barry, and asked him to sit at her desk so they could both look at the staff's profiles. There were several changes he suggested and worked on making new profiles for every employee. The previous IT person had gotten sloppy, and Barry was recently assigned Chessmore Industries as a client in the last month after the other gentleman had been moved to a different spot in the company. He spent much of the day in her office changing profiles and setting up different rights. Most of the employees wouldn't notice a change, but she certainly hoped the person taking her money would. She made sure Barry knew it was imperative to keep most of her employees from having access to her financials and bank accounts. Edna even made sure Doris had no access to her financial information, and since she really never had an interest in learning that part of the business she didn't think Doris would even notice. Once Barry completed Edna's office, he started on her other entities. It went quicker once he knew how she wanted the profiles set. While he was working away at her desk, Doris knocked on the door frame and entered the room.

"Yes, Doris?"

Doris looked at Barry and then back at Edna. "I just wondered if you needed anything else today. If not, I'll leave early."

"No, nothing. I'll see you tomorrow." Doris hesitated. "Do you need something else, Doris?"

"No, I just wondered if we're being hacked or something. He's been here a long time."

"No. I'm having trouble with my computer. I probably opened an email I shouldn't have. A little rusty, you know. Then he noticed I needed an upgrade."

"Oh. Okay then. Good luck. See you tomorrow." Doris looked at Barry then left for the day.

Barry leaned back in the chair. "Quick thinking."

"Do you think she noticed the changes already?"

"She might have. I can give you that answer tomorrow when I look at the server. I can tell who has attempted to get into the files so I can monitor that for a while and let you know who is trying. I have a few more to do, but I can do that from my own office. If I have any questions, I'll call you." He hit print and gave her a copy of all of her employees. "Let me know if I missed anyone, but as far as I can see, HR does a nice job getting them loaded. I just hope I didn't delete someone I shouldn't have. Some of the employees had already been deactivated, so I deleted their profiles completely. No one is letting me know to set up an original profile. I'll fix it so HR will have to call me before the employee is given access to any files. Sound good to you?"

"Wonderful. Thank you so much."

"No problem. That's what you pay me for."

Edna reviewed her list carefully, noting names of staff she had never met. That was going to change as soon as she could get things settled at the office. She used to make rounds of all her offices and businesses quarterly, and she was long overdue.

Doris questioned her the following day about her computer, and she reassured her that the computer was running well now. Barry did spend some time working on her personal computer checking it for malware and setting up a virus protection program for her. He could monitor it from his office and would be able to tell if someone was attempting to get into her files.

In the meantime, the CPA called her back and said everything from her husband's accounts looked right and no one had been dipping into the actual accounts. Carson explained that there was a leak only on the Chessmore Industries side which helped eliminate one problem and narrow things down for her to investigate.

A little after two, she told Doris she was leaving for the day to run some errands. Edna locked up her desk and made sure she had both sets of keys. The copies of her financials and the employee profiles were now locked up tight. She drove out of the garage, waved at the attendant, and headed downtown. She hadn't seen any loiterers since she told the attendant about the incident.

It would be difficult to find a parking spot this time of day, so she wanted to make sure she had plenty of time to make it to Jindels. Jordan wanted her there early and waiting, and she aimed to oblige. She finally found a place close to her personal hairdresser and a few shops she liked to visit occasionally. Edna got out and fed the meter to last for a couple of hours and walked into the hairdressers to make an appointment.

Her hair had gotten so long and unmanageable, she continued to tie it back into a pony tail. It really wasn't a good style for her or her age group. They took one look at her and immediately set her up for an appointment later that afternoon. She chuckled as she thought of the look on their faces when she walked in.

Edna headed on down the street window shopping as she went along. She finally noticed that someone following her. She tried to get a good look at him but to no avail. Edna angled herself so she could try to get a look at the reflection in the window, but it did no good. When she arrived at the next dress shop, she finally went inside because by then the hair was standing on the back of her neck and she was becoming quite nervous. Edna went to the first rack and held up a shirt while looking out the window.

Whoever was following her remained just out of sight. She walked to a rack on the other side of the room and repeated the process, but she still couldn't see him. A clerk walked up and asked if she could help her. Edna was so surprised, that she shrieked, which in turn scared the clerk and she yelped.

The clerk reached out to Edna. "I'm so sorry."

"No, I'm sorry to have scared you. I was just so intent on something, I didn't see or hear you come up to me."

"Can I help you find something?"

Edna was still taking some calming breaths. "Actually, maybe so. I think someone is following me, but I can't see them from here. I don't want them to know I saw them. Do you think you could tell me what he is wearing or what he looks like?"

"I see." The clerk looked around.

"No, not in here. Outside. Could you go outside and pretend to look in the window or something?"

The clerk was intrigued by the mystery. "I'm game." The clerk wandered over to the display and adjusted a dress, then went out the door to look at the display. She looked around outside and came back into the store. "There isn't anyone right outside of the store, and I didn't see anyone standing on either side. Are you sure you are being followed?"

Edna nodded and moved to the middle of the store and looked out the window. The only person she thought it could be was someone leaning against a lamppost across the street talking on a phone and smoking. She asked the clerk to use her phone to take a picture of him. The clerk managed to get a couple of pictures for her and handed the phone back for review.

"Strange. I've never met him before."
"Do you know why you're being followed?"
"I have no idea. Someone was in my yard the other day too."
"You better call the cops."
"I guess so. Thank you for all of your help today." Edna looked around and then at her watch. "I don't have time right now, but I'll be back to shop another day. I love the style of your clothes."

Edna scooted out the door and down the street in a rush. Jindels was on the other side of the street, and as she turned to cross, she saw the man start crossing to her side. She waited until the last minute and crossed just before a truck came by. She rushed into Jindels and stopped to catch her breath.

Stepping back into the darkness, she looked back out the door. The man was busy looking for her and was going to cross back over the street soon. She turned and found a booth toward the back and scooted in toward the wall with her back to the door, hunched down so her head wouldn't show. She waved to the bartender and shook her head, hoping he understood. Edna tried to slow her breathing down and relax. She heard the door open and murmuring at the bar. Another minute went by and the door opened again. She began to relax and looked at her watch. It was almost three.

Pretty soon, a gruff-looking man stood by the booth with a drink and slid in. She gasped, but he quickly raised a finger to his lips to quiet her. Edna realized it must be Jordan, so she got out her phone and showed him the picture. He nodded, and they sat there without talking, him enjoying his drink. She used her hand to show him the drink sign, and he nodded. Jordan went back to the bar. He returned with a second drink of his own and a glass of water. After about fifteen minutes, the other man left, and Edna sighed in relief when Jordan announced he was gone.

"Thank God. I was so scared."
"Who is he?"
"I have no idea. I just knew he was following me."
"Send me his picture." Edna was shaking so badly that he took her phone and sent it to himself.
"Let me get you a real drink. What do you want?"
"Do they have wine?"
"I can check."
"Any red will do. Make it a large glass."

Jordan went to get the best wine they carried. He brought the whole bottle back with him and poured her a large glass. She gulped it down, and he poured another one but stopped her from drinking it.

"Just hold on. I need you sober enough to drive home." She nodded and only took a sip. "Okay. Spill. What is going on?"

She started from the beginning when George died suddenly and she was out of commission for six months.

"Now I'm back to work, and when I went over my financial reports I found a lot of discrepancies."

"What have you done so far?"

"First, I went to see my CPA Carson Shoemaker. He gave me your card. I took his advice on several things. I had my IT guy come in, and we reworked the staff profiles throughout my businesses. Carson suggested I call you to see if you could find out who was embezzling my money by checking to see if anyone has suddenly been living beyond their means or if they are gambling it away. My IT man, Barry, says he will keep an eye on the server and will let me know if he sees anything unusual since he reworked the system. Now all of a sudden, I'm being followed, except maybe it isn't all of a sudden. I thought someone was in my backyard the other day, and some homeless guy knocked on my window in the parking garage at work to ask me for money. Now I'm not so sure it was a homeless guy."

Jordan took a drink and let Edna catch her breath. "Mrs. Chessmore, it sounds right up my alley. I'll have to thank Carson for the business. I think it is more important to figure out who is following you, but I can check on your employees too. The IT guy can probably track that culprit down faster than I can, but I'll do what I can. Do you have a list of employees?"

"Not on me. I wanted to see if you took the job first."

"I'll stop by the office tomorrow disguised as a salesman, and I'll get the list then, plus it will give me a chance to look around. Where are you going from here?"

"I'm parked a couple of blocks down in front of my hairdressers. I have an appointment scheduled pretty soon, then I'm headed for home."

"You cross the street, and I'll follow you from this side. If it looks like you're in danger, I'll join you. Otherwise, I will wait and follow you home. You won't see me. Take another drink and enjoy the haircut."

"Thank you. I have to go. Oh, wait. We didn't discuss your fee."

"When I come by tomorrow, we will take care of that part of our business. I know the building you're in. I'll see you tomorrow."

Jordan downed his drink, took what was left of the wine to the bartender, and paid the bill. He watched as Edna took off for her appointment, and shortly thereafter a man followed. He ambled down the street, casually keeping an eye on everyone, and made sure she was safe.

After Edna went into the hairdressers, the tail stopped to talk to another man briefly. One left and the other one went to his own car to wait. It was conveniently parked two slots down from Edna's. Jordan knew he had plenty of time and walked the two blocks to his car and drove around until he could locate a parking spot a block away from them both. He sat back and waited.

An hour later, all three cars were headed toward Edna's house. The traffic was terrible, which helped Jordan stay hidden behind them all. When she got to the residential sections and the traffic thinned, Jordan pulled back farther but managed to keep an eye on both cars. Edna gave him her home address, and as he got closer he pulled back farther so he wouldn't be noticed as they all slowed down.

Edna pulled into her drive, and the tail did a U-turn and parked across the street from the gate. Jordan drove by and thought to himself, *"Amateurs."* Jordan sat back a block and watched. By nine o'clock, the tail left the house and Jordan went home, but not before he called the police on the plate. Stolen.

Just before lunch, Doris knocked on Edna's door and announced a visitor. "It's a salesman, and he said you were expecting him. Here's his card. Just so you know, I didn't make an appointment for him. Did you?"
Edna took the card and smiled. "Yes, Doris. I did. Please send him in."

Doris frowned, went back out the door, and directed the man into the office. She left the door ajar and went to her desk. The man turned around and shut the door tight, noting Doris's shocked face before it closed.

"Do you have a radio?" Edna nodded toward her bookshelf. Jordan walked over and turned it on just loud enough to cover up their voices. He sat down and spoke quietly as he handed a file over to Edna. She reached into her desk and exchanged the paperwork with her own. As she read his contract, Jordan waited. She nodded, signed the contract, and got her personal checkbook out of her purse to pay his retainer.

Jordan explained what he saw when he followed her home. "I'm working on who it is, but the plate is stolen. I also have that picture you sent me. In the meantime, here is another business card. I think you should hire a bodyguard. I called him and he can take you on right now, but you need to make the call, not me. The man needs to be by your side at all times. That means driving you back and forth to work and anywhere in between. Don't go anywhere without him. He will need to live with you until all of this is over. You can pretend he is your driver, but he will protect you. You may have a bug in here, so that's why I wanted the radio on. He can look for the bugs and get rid of them. Plus, you don't need Miss Nosy out there to hear anything."

"I understand. So you think I'm in danger?"

"Honey, as long as you have a tail, there is a danger. I don't know what from, but someone is out there watching you." She sighed. "I'll start running the checks on your employees this afternoon. It would be nice if you could tell me where to start though."

"I have no clue."

"All right, I'll just start at the top of the list. You call Mike right away. I've been tailing the guy tailing you, but I won't be able to get any other work done if I'm doing that all the time. We may have to bring in additional help depending on what we find in these files."

"I'll give him a call right away. I just hope we can get this all figured out so I can go on with my life." Jordan nodded, told her to leave the radio on, grabbed his file, and left the room, leaving the door wide open.

Doris came running in. "What did he want?"

"He's a salesman, Doris. What do you think he wanted?"

"Well, that was rude shutting the door like that." She looked over at the radio. "What's that on for?" She walked over to shut it off.

"Leave it," Edna said sharply.

Doris jumped. "I'm sorry. You never have it on."

"Well, I do now." Doris looked hurt.

"I'm sorry, Doris. I have a touch of a headache."
"Well, maybe the radio noise is bothering you. I can shut it off."
"Doris, please go back to your desk and shut the door on your way out."

Frustrated, Doris stalked out of the room and tried not to slam the door in anger. Edna felt guilty about her tone of voice, but she had never known Doris to be so nosy or bossy. She picked up the phone number Jordan gave her and used her cell phone to make the call.

"Mike here."
"Edna Chessmore here," she said quietly.
"I got it. I will be there around five. Don't go anywhere."
"Okay. Thanks."

Mike hung up. Although they didn't discuss anything over the phone, and since Jordan mentioned a bug, she thought it was a good idea nothing was said. Edna went to the window and watched the traffic for a while. As she focused more on the sidewalk, she noticed a man across the street just standing there watching her building. On occasion, he would pace back and forth and talk on the phone, but he mostly kept his eyes on the building. *"Crazy people."* Frustrated, she went to the door and opened it. Doris was on the phone with her back to Edna. She listened as Doris spoke quietly to someone.

"I don't know what she's doing. She's acting weird or paranoid." Doris swirled her chair around and noticed Edna standing at the doorway watching her. "I have to go." She quickly hung up the phone and looked back to Edna, seeing her frown. "Mrs. Chessmore. What can I do for you?"

"How about you go get me some lunch downstairs? I'll give you enough to get something for yourself too."

"That's okay. I brought my own today, but I'll run down and get something for you. What do you want?"

"Just a small salad, and if they have their breadsticks today, get me two or three of those." She handed Doris a ten. "Are you sure you don't want me to buy you anything?"

"Nope, I'm just fine. I have leftovers today. I'll be right back."

"Thank you, Doris. I'm sorry for snapping at you earlier."

"That's all right. Headaches can do that to a person, and you've been working pretty hard since you got back."

Doris took off for the elevator, and Edna went back to her office window. The same man was standing there talking on the phone. After hanging up, he walked down the street, and just before she lost sight of him he got in a car. She breathed a sigh of relief until she realized a new person was lounging against the same pole. She got out her phone and zoomed in to take a picture. The focus wasn't very good from that distance and angle, but she thought it was good enough. She sent the picture to Jordan with a text, *"Another one. Mike coming."*

The afternoon dragged on, and Edna alternately sat at her desk and fidgeted or stared out her window and watched her watcher. Doris continued to keep an eye on her without trying to be noticed. Finally, Edna had enough.

"Doris. It's almost five, so you can call it a day. I'll lock up when I leave."

"It's okay. I can stay until five."

Edna looked at her square in the eye. "Doris, I believe I asked you to leave. I won't dock your pay for leaving early. Just go."

Doris jumped up and grabbed her purse. "Fine." She stormed off mumbling about how she didn't need to be bossed around.

Edna went back to looking out her office window. It was some time before she noticed Doris's car leave the garage and watched it speed down the street. In the background, she could hear other staff leaving the floor for the day. Her radio was grating on her already-tight nerves by the time the five o'clock news started. She felt more than heard someone come to her door. She could see a reflection in the window and slowly turned around. In the doorway was a very tall, large man. He immediately raised a finger to his lips to keep her quiet. He pointed a thumb to himself and mouthed *"Mike."* She nodded, relieved. He looked like a force to be reckoned with.

He put his briefcase on her desk and quietly took out some equipment. She went back to her window and he shut her door. Mike began to check for bugs while she watched the man on the street. A new one arrived, so Edna took a picture and sent it to Jordan. *"Another one. Mike here."*

Mike finished the office and moved out to Doris's desk area. She sat back down and watched him methodically search every nook and cranny possible. When he completed his job, he came back to her desk with a glass of water that held several small black objects.

"I assume you found what you were looking for?"
"I did."
"And now they know you did too."
"Correct."
"Next step?"
"Watch."

She spent the next hour watching him install small objects in her office. One by Doris's desk, a couple in her office, and throughout the rest of the office area. One faced the elevator. He continued to look for bugs while he worked and found a few more.

"How much of this floor is yours?"
"All of it."
"I'll be back."

An hour later, Edna's nerves were completely on edge, but Mike finally returned.

"Okay. Now down to business. First of all, I've got my security cameras and bugs all over the office now, and I can record everything that goes on right here."

He pointed to something that looked just like her radio. Mike walked over to her radio and unplugged it, then replaced it with his gadget. He turned it on, and asked her what channel she had been listening to, then set it.

"Now, you still have a radio, but I recommend you turn it off when you leave so I can get a clear recording in case they come back. It will record right here in this office and also on my laptop no matter where I am. I'll leave the laptop at your house most of the time. Are you ready for me to stay?"

"I didn't call and tell the staff to get a room ready yet because of the possible bugs."

"Good. Do you think your staff can be trusted?"

"They've been with me for years and have stuck by me through the worst of times."

"Jordan will be checking on them, you know," Mike said. "You will have to tell them I'm your bodyguard."

"The staff already knows I thought I saw someone in the yard. With three widows in the house, they will probably feel safer, too."

Mike helped her make sure everything was locked tight before leaving. They rode the elevator down. "We're going to take my car and leave yours here for now. I'll have it picked up later and taken to a mechanic shop. It will explain me driving you every day and staying at the house. Wait here a second." Mike walked into the garage and looked around. The attendant was looking at his phone, and Mike didn't see anyone else. He motioned for her to follow and he quickly took her to his car. "If we're lucky, no one will notice you in my car tonight. They'll wonder what happened to you and see your car still in the garage." He laughed as they drove out of the garage and down the street.

Once they arrived at the house, Mike pulled the car into the garage. He immediately got his equipment out and started checking the garage, and then as they entered the house, with each step, he continued into each room. She led him to her den, and as he worked she closed the drapes and turned on the music.

He smiled at her as he continued to work throughout the room. "I think we're clean in here, but I'll continue to monitor every room. Then I will go outside tomorrow and make a sweep. You better have your staff come in here since I'll be wandering around all the rooms in the house."

Edna went to the kitchen and asked Martha and Sarah to come to the den. "Ladies, this is Mike. I hired him to be my bodyguard."

The two looked shocked, and Martha reached out to grab Sarah. "It's true, you have seen someone outside."

"Yes, and they have been following me and watching me at work." The women gasped. "Mike is going to live here as long as we need him. He will take me back and forth to work and keep an eye on me at all times. Now, he needs to tell you what he'll be doing next."

"Ladies, I have to check every room in the place for bugs. If one of you could accompany me to make sure I check every room, I would appreciate it."

"I have dinner almost ready," Sarah spoke up.

"Martha, you take him, but start in the kitchen and dining room so we can eat when it's ready."

Edna sat in a wingback chair and relaxed for the first time that day. She kept thinking of Doris and her strange behavior. She didn't know if it was because she, herself, was stressed or Doris didn't appreciate her boss coming back to work. Sarah hollered it was time for supper, so she quit her wool-gathering and headed for the dining room. Sarah had outdone herself since she had company and proved she could fix a great meal on short notice.

The four of them sat down, and Edna told them of the recent events. She even explained about having a private investigator hired. Martha and Sarah were pretty wrapped up in the mystery and started throwing out suggestions as to whom and why Edna was being followed. Mike and Edna both laughed as the women each tried to outdo the other with outlandish tales and stories of intrigue. After dessert, Edna asked Martha to fix up a spare room on the main floor for Mike while she walked with him to finish the electronic check of the home.

"Before we continue, do you have a security system?"

"No." She shook her head. "George refused to have one, and I haven't given any thought to adding one."

"Can you afford one?"

"Yes, I'm sure I can. Do you have a specific company in mind?"

"Of course."

"And, of course, they will come right out if you call."

"Of course," Mike said.

"I think you boys all stick together and see how much

money you can get from the widow ladies. Speaking of which, you haven't told me how much I owe you." He pulled a contract out of his pocket, and she read as he worked. While completing the last room on the main floor, she went to the den and wrote him a check. "Here's your retainer. Don't spend it all in one place."

"Thanks." He stuck it in his shirt pocket and told Edna he was done with the main floor and it was clean. He was ready to go upstairs.

"Can you please wait until tomorrow to do the upstairs?" Edna asked. "I'm exhausted."

"No problem. I don't expect any issues since the main floor was clean."

Martha arrived and told Mike his suite was ready. He went back to the car for his bag and followed her to his room. It would certainly meet his needs as it was almost like a studio apartment. He had been in there to sweep the room for electronics but had no idea this suite would be his new living quarters. After Martha left, he set up his computer and checked the video at Edna's office. Assured it was quiet, he called Jordan to check in. Jordan didn't like the fact that whoever was following Edna had multiple people and multiple cars. The license plates he ran on all the cars he followed were stolen. He would continue to try to identify the men she had taken pictures of. They both agreed that Edna was a pretty sharp client and didn't appear to panic. She'd been through a lot and didn't deserve the trauma she was going through now.

Jordan already checked out her staff and was working diligently on the long list of employees. So far everyone checked out, but he was just getting started. Mike felt reassured the house hadn't been tampered with but needed to complete both the upstairs and the perimeter the next day. Once he got Edna to the office, he would return and finish up.

Edna stood drinking coffee by the window in the kitchen while Sarah fixed breakfast. "Sarah, could you fix me a light lunch every day? I won't be free to go out right now."

"Yes, ma'am. I'll be happy to."

Mike could smell breakfast cooking and found his way back to the kitchen. Pouring himself some coffee, he walked over beside Edna and looked out the window. "Anything of interest?"

"Not really. I seem to spend a lot of time looking out windows. Would you walk me through the rose garden this morning before breakfast? I miss doing that every day."

"Yes, ma'am. I will be right back." Mike was only gone a short time before returning to her side. She was slightly taken aback when she noticed the shoulder holster.

"Just a precaution, Mrs. Chessmore."

She nodded, and they refilled their coffee before Edna took her casual walk in the garden, bending to smell the roses on occasion. She felt satisfied that they were doing well, and her trimming from the other day still looked good. Once inside, they had a hearty breakfast before leaving for the office. Sarah put together a few items for her lunch and threw in a snack just in case she worked late. Mike reassured both Martha and Sarah they were not being watched themselves and to go on with their daily lives as if nothing was going on. He sure didn't want them to cause any more suspicion upon Edna. He also mentioned someone would be coming by soon to install an electronic security system, but he would make sure he was there when they arrived and supervise the installation.

Edna walked through the lobby with Mike at her side, startling the main receptionist. She hadn't been there when Mike showed up at Edna's office the day before. Mike was six feet two, dark hair, and burly. The man's presence led anyone to believe he shouldn't be messed with. He frowned at the receptionist, and she visibly shrank from the glare.

After getting on the elevator, she grinned. "Do you like causing grief and discontent wherever you go?"

"Yes, ma'am, I certainly do. That's why I've lived so long."

"How old are you?"

"Fifty-eight."

"Really? I'm surprised."

"Why?"

"I don't know. I hadn't really thought about it before, but I guess I just assumed you were quite a bit younger. No gray hair, and you are in pretty good shape."

Just as the elevator opened, he whispered, "Dye job."

She laughed as they walked toward her office, leaving everyone gaping behind her. "Good morning, Doris. This is Mike. You will be seeing a lot more of him from now on."

Doris stammered as they walked by. "Y-yes, Mrs. Chessmore."

"Thank you, Mike. That was an enjoyable walk this morning."

"You're very welcome, Mrs. Chessmore. I enjoyed

the roses myself. I can see why you like them."

"Oh. The roses. Yes, that too, but I meant through the office building. I'll see you this evening."

"Yes, you will, Mrs. Chessmore. I'll be back at five."

He did an informal salute as he left and frowned at Doris to fluster her again just for the fun of it. Edna predicted as soon as Mike left, Doris would come running in, and she didn't disappoint her.

"Mrs. Chessmore, who is that?"
"I told you, his name is Mike."
"I know, but why?"
"Why is his name Mike? I assume his mother called him that."

Doris was completely frustrated with her boss. She wanted to yell at her but took a deep breath and calmed down. "Mrs. Chessmore, may I ask what Mike's position is?"

"Oh sure, you may ask." Edna stood looking at Doris. For some reason, she really felt like goading Doris this morning and was getting a kick out of it. She figured Mike was rubbing off on her already.

"Mrs. Chessmore," Doris said in a huff, "I don't know what has come over you lately. I really don't." With that, she turned and went back to her desk leaving the question unanswered.

Edna turned and smiled. Sitting at her desk, she checked her emails and phone messages and then remembered to turn on the radio so it would distract anyone listening to her calls. When she flipped it on, she could see Doris look at her and shake her head before returning to her own work. Edna decided she was caught up with her office work and needed to start visiting with her managers at their locations. She also needed to do a little investigative work in her own office. She got up and went to Doris's desk.

"What are you working on?"
Doris jumped. "Oh. You scared me. I'm typing the reports for the last board meeting."
"Make sure I get a copy. Why wasn't I at those meetings, Doris?"
"Um, you were gone?"
"I'm back now, so set up a special meeting for me. Once it's scheduled, please get it on my calendar."
"Yes, ma'am."

She walked through the office to see her other employees. Some were playing on their phones, and others saw her coming and went right to work. She frowned at the overabundance of staff. "*Why do I need so many people if they have time to play on their phones and sit around?*" At each desk, she asked them what their job title was and what they did for Chessmore Industries. She began to write everything down, and as she completed her tour, she got everyone's attention.

"The economy is a little tight right now. I need to know if I'm getting my money's worth from each and every one of you. I want a time study done for each day for a week. I want to know what each one of you is doing for Chessmore Industries, how long it takes, and if you have any free time. If we don't have enough to keep you busy, we could possibly line you up to work for one of the other growing organizations in our company. When I walked in, I saw several of you on your cell phones. I'm not paying for you to play on your phones. Keep in mind that if you have work to do, then get it done or else you can find the door. Now. Does anyone have any questions?"

A young man stood up with his phone in his hand and ear buds around his neck. "I like to play music while I work if that's okay with you."

"That's fine unless it becomes distracting to others around you. I've been turning on my own radio lately." She took a peek at Doris who continued to frown. "Anyone else?"

"Are you going to fire anyone? I can't afford to be without my job."

"If you aren't doing your job or doing it well, we might have to discuss those options. You were all hired to do a specific job, and I expect you to do it to the best of your abilities. If you don't like your job, quit. As I said, if I need to move your job to a different entity, I will. The offices are all within driving distance of each other, so it shouldn't be a burden to anyone if that happens. As long as you all stay busy and keep up the excellent work you have done in the past, there won't be any issues." She turned to Doris. "Doris?"

"Mrs. Chessmore?"

"I'll be driving out to my other offices sometime this week. What will you be doing while I'm gone?"

"Ummm, what do you want me to do?"

Edna frowned. "Your time study, just like everyone else."

Doris straightened her shoulders and glared at her. Edna was beginning to think Doris would be one of the first to go if she continued this attitude. She also planned to get with Mike each evening and review the tapes to see what the staff did when she was out of the office.

"Oh, before I go back to my office, let me remind you that I'm a fair employer. I'm sure you will agree you receive excellent wages and benefits. It's up to you to decide if you earn this job. I'll know in a week. Thank you for all you do. There is no reason to suspect I won't be happy with your time studies. Just be honest and thorough."

Edna went back to her office. She could almost guarantee she would be either letting a couple of people go or they would quit. The disinterest in some of their faces was obvious. Doris, on the other hand, probably had free rein while she was gone, and now she had to work again. It will be an interesting week.

Mike finished checking the house, including the basement and attic. He wandered the grounds using his sophisticated equipment. It wasn't until he arrived at the front gate that he picked up an alarm there was a bug. He finally found a small camera and speaker facing the gate. He removed it, crushed it, and continued working outside the gated property. *"Amateurs".* He then left but stood close by the front gate and remained in the shadows. If anyone came to check on the camera, he wanted to be there. His own security crew would arrive first thing in the morning, and he would have to check the perimeter occasionally until Mrs. Chessmore's security was up and running.

After an hour of waiting, he had to head back to get Mrs. Chessmore. He had her car picked up that morning and taken to a mechanic shop owned by his brother who would hold it until Mike and Jordan thought it safe for her to drive again. Mike arrived to get Edna at five sharp. The office building was emptying quickly, and he had to wait some time for an elevator to go up. When the doors opened, he scared Doris, who was just leaving. He frowned at her, and she let out a yelp and took off.

Mike chuckled as he got on and pushed the button to go up. Just before the doors closed, another man got on and pushed a button for the floor below Edna's. He glanced at him and had the feeling something wasn't quite right. He took out his phone, fiddled with it, and took a picture of the man as Mike cleared his throat to cover the sound of the camera. The man got off on his floor, and Mike continued to Edna's floor. He met Edna in her office and showed her the picture. They compared it to the ones on her phone and agreed it wasn't any of them, but she had never seen him before either.

"I'll make sure the cameras are actively working. Hang on." He connected to an app on his phone and worked through each of the cameras in the office. "Looks like they are all in the right place. I have an idea that what I'm about to do isn't very legal." He went to the fire escape door and worked on it for a while. Satisfied, he shut the door tight. "I think that will take care of it."
"What did you do?"
"I made sure no one can get in from the stairwell. You can get out but not in. Does anyone use it to walk the stairs for exercise?"
"Are you kidding me? Not in this building."

"Good. No one will notice except us. Just a minute." Mike scrolled through his app again and adjusted the angle of the camera before closing the app. "It focuses on the door of the fire escape window so we can see who is trying to get the door open. Most people will look through the window to see what the obstruction is. Once we are downstairs, I'll deactivate the button for your floor on all the elevators until seven in the morning."

"I can't believe you can do stuff like that."

"Just trying to keep you safe, Mrs. Chessmore."

She shrugged. "If you say so. I'll leave all that techy stuff to you."

They rode down the elevator, and once they were standing in the lobby, Mike had Edna act like she was talking on her phone while he created his magic. He opened the elevator to make sure the button for her floor wouldn't work and allowed the doors to close again. He offered an imperceptible nod, and Edna pretended to end her call. "I'm ready, Mike." He nodded and led her through the lobby and to his car. Mike had a silent alarm on his car that would notify him if anyone touched it. That way, he was assured of his client's safety and his. More than once over the years that alarm kept him alive.

They zipped through the traffic, and Mike managed several twists and turns before going to the house. If he had someone following them, he wanted to make it worth their trouble to keep up. Once he entered the driveway, he figured someone else would be watching anyway. He drove slowly down Edna's street and noted two different cars. One was Jordan, and he was watching the other car. He smiled as he turned into the driveway and waited for the gate to open.

They headed straight into the garage, and once inside the house, he told Edna he was headed back outside. He grabbed his equipment and checked the gate area once again, took down a new bug, and destroyed it. Then he walked the perimeter and found no other surveillance equipment before standing in the shadows and waiting for something to happen. He felt his phone vibrate, and it was Jordan texting that the man was on the move.

Mike watched as the stranger came up to the gate and looked for his equipment. Not finding it, he stomped off, calling someone on the way to his car. The car drove off, and soon after Jordan followed. Mike went back to the house to keep an eye on his client.

The security company arrived the following morning before Mike left to take Edna to work. He showed them the perimeter and then the grounds. He wanted new motion lights installed in strategic areas along with cameras everywhere. There would be a new gate entrance code, too. After Edna asked Mike to take her to her other offices in town and to stay with her through the day, he needed to get the security company moving and make sure they knew what he wanted done.

When they left the house, Mike drove as if he was going to her office but veered off into the heavy traffic and lost their tail. They walked into the headquarters of her cleaning company and were taken directly to the manager. The place was exceptionally clean and modestly furnished. She introduced Mike, and he stayed in the background as the discussions of how the business was being handled. The growth of the company continued, and the staff were mostly women. The established work hours for office buildings and businesses were usually after closing, and that was when mothers could leave their children with their spouses or parents. The staff's wages stretched farther, and it made for happier employees. Many of the men who were hired were trained to run the cleaning equipment for stripping floors and waxing. Most of the women had difficulty with the equipment due to needing more upper-body strength. Even at that, everyone was given the option to try any available job, and the manager waited for the employee to pick the area they felt most comfortable with day in and day out.

Once the employees proved themselves, they could ask for a transfer to another position as they became available. Some of the employees liked to rotate in and out of jobs and just went where the work was, no matter what day it was. The manager was very flexible with her staff, and her low staff turnover rate showed the loyalty they had for the company. Back in the office, they discussed the financials once more and looked at the budget. Everything seemed as it should be, and her staffing ratio was right on track. Stopping to talk to the staff in the accounting office didn't bring up any concerns, either.

"You keep adding contracts and staff to fill the spots. With managers like you, I don't have to worry about the business. Good job and keep up the hard work. You run a well-oiled machine here. I'm ashamed to say my own staff doesn't work as hard."

Edna shook hands and felt comfortable about leaving her manager running Chessmore Cleaning Industries. Mike stopped by a fast-food place and ordered them both a sandwich and drinks. It was nice enough that they parked out back and sat at a table outside under some trees. Mike kept a close eye on the surroundings out of habit, but he knew that their tail had lost their car hours ago. Edna closed her eyes and lifted her face to the sun. Mike watched her relax and enjoy the outdoors. He vowed to get her out in her own yard more, especially her rose garden.

That afternoon, they drove over to the laundry division, and again she noted the place was clean and well-kept. As Edna toured the huge laundry facility itself, she noted that everyone was wearing their ear guards and the cooling system worked well. Where appropriate, the staff also wore their protective eyeglasses. Throughout the area, there were large fans to help move the air to keep the working temperature appropriate. There were a variety of age groups working at the facility, and the manager prided himself on having a high retention rate of employees.

In the office, they discussed the financials and whether or not the budget was sufficient. The staffing ratio was right on, but the manager discussed the need for some unexpected repairs.

"It isn't in the budget to get that particular equipment replaced this year, but I don't know how long we can keep the current machine working. Every time it goes down, it slows our productivity."

"I appreciate you trying to keep it going. Let's look at it this way. If you order it now, it will take a while to get it in and installed. Look at the list of things that are in the budget and see if you can push them to next year. When you make your monthly report to the board, make a note that we discussed it and decided for the sake of the business and productivity, we need to go over budget. I want you to bring the list of every piece of machinery and their age to the board. We may have to increase your budget for next year, and the more contracts you get, the bigger your budget needs to be. Maybe we aren't giving you enough money or equipment to work with to grow efficiently."

On the drive to her office, she became thoughtful. "It looks like I'm the one that isn't being proficient. I let it all get away from me, and my office staff got lazy."

Mike listened but didn't comment. His mind was on the tail. Mike parked the car and asked Edna if she'd be all right to go up to the office on her own while he watched the parking garage. She reassured him she would be fine. Edna went on through the building entrance, and Mike stood behind a pillar across from his car. A car pulled in and parked six cars down. He walked quietly behind it and got the plate number and make of the car. He then sent a text to Jordan. Every car so far had a stolen plate, but it didn't hurt to try again. A few minutes later, Jordan texted back. *"Cops on the way."* Mike stood back and watched. Ten minutes later, cruisers pulled up to block the car in, and guns were drawn. The man did as he was told and put his hands on the steering wheel. While they were all busy, Mike casually walked into the building and rode up to Edna's office.

As he walked by Doris's desk, she jumped. "Why so jumpy, Miss?"

"You're always sneaking up on me."

"Really?" He grinned and went into Edna's office. She was just hanging up the phone.

"I've taken care of all my messages, and I'm ready to go home." She shut off the radio and grabbed her purse, checked to make sure her desk was locked and the computer was off, and walked with Mike to the elevator. "Did you look at the video last evening?" Edna asked.

"I did. Want to see it?"

"Yes, I do. Especially after seeing everyone else being so proficient in their own offices."

"We'll review it after supper," Mike said. That way, we can sit without being distracted."

By the time they got back to his car, the police were gone and so was the driver of the car. He didn't say a word to Edna. After supper, they went to the den and Mike set up his laptop. He showed her how he could look at several areas at once or just one specific area. He first focused on the stairwell fire door, and as he predicted, someone's face appeared in the window as he tried to open it. The man became angry and hit the door a few times before leaving. It was the man with whom Mike rode in the elevator with, just as he figured. Edna couldn't help but chuckle.

"If nothing else, you are going to provide me evening entertainment."

She asked to see her staff video. It probably wasn't the most ethical thing to do since she hadn't let them know she was starting to video them, but she had to get to the bottom of the embezzlement. He put the video on fast-forward so they could get through several hours of the video quickly. Most of her staff appeared to be working except for the two she pegged for being lazy. The most disappointing was her secretary. Filing her nails, chatting on her own phone, and who knew what else she was doing while sitting back with her feet on the desk. Edna decided to ask for Doris's time study review the following day.

"You let me know if anything exciting happen tonight. Tomorrow, I'm going to need a new secretary."

Mike finished looking at the video after Edna left the room, then switched over to Edna's house. He had most of the perimeter set up and under surveillance now, and the crew would return the following day to wire the house. He sent Jordan a text and found out he was across the street watching another car. *"Called the cops."* Mike laughed. Pretty soon, he hoped someone sang like a canary on who they were working for. This was the fourth car Jordan called the police about, plus the one Mike turned in from the garage. It was a good thing they were friends with the local police department.

The following day, Edna stayed home and watched the security crew finish wiring her house. They hooked up the monitors in her den and put them behind a lovely cabinet. No one would see them if she had company. Until Mike was no longer needed, he would still have access to all her security. After the job was done, she would change the access code. Martha and Sarah were both given the temporary code so they could come and go at will.

Mike went through the office video again and laughed because when Edna wasn't in the office, Doris did absolutely nothing except answer the phone occasionally. When she was on her own phone, someone else answered the business line. The rest of the staff would frown and point at her occasionally as they talked among themselves. This was not going to bode well for Doris.

"Mrs. Chessmore, when you're ready to go to the office, let me know. I need to do some work in my room first."

Mike pulled up the video from the camera on Doris and copied it to a thumb drive. Edna was ready at the same time as Mike, and they met in the hallway. It was late in the afternoon, but she planned to talk to Doris before the end of the day and see what she had to say about her current behavior. They arrived just as Doris was picking up her purse to leave. It was four thirty, not five. Doris quickly put her purse down and sat back at her desk. Edna asked her to follow her into the office and to bring in her time study.

Doris jerked as if slapped. "My time study?"

"Yes. I want to see what you've been working on so far."

"Ummm."

Doris shuffled papers around on her desk trying to bide some time while waiting for Edna to go to her office. Edna gave up waiting on Doris and went to her desk, but Mike remained standing close by. Doris became extremely agitated and finally gave up and walked into the office with Mike following her and shutting the door. At the click of the door, Doris jumped again.

"Sit down, please. Since your hands are empty, I assume you don't have anything written down."

"Well, it wasn't supposed to be due until next week."

"I see. So tell me exactly what you were going to write out since evidently you can remember what you do each day."

Doris turned red, not from embarrassment, but from

anger. "I've been running this office just fine while you've been gone. You never answered any calls, so I just took over. Now you are questioning my ability to do my job. You sit in here with your little radio going and looking out the window while I slave away out there and do your job."

Edna was appalled at Doris's behavior, and her face showed it. She tried to control her own anger. "So tell me. When I'm out of the office, you handle everything efficiently and that is why Chessmore Industries is doing so well?"

"Yes, exactly."

"Were you handling the financials too?"

"I was trying, but you know I'm not very good at it. Now you have me locked out of there and several other places, and I can't do my job."

"I see. Hold on a second."

Edna turned her computer on when she entered the room to check her emails, and conveniently there was one from Barry telling her who was trying to get into the financial files. Doris's name was first with several attempts. There were a couple of other attempts by others, but nothing compared to what Doris was doing.

"Interesting. Yes, I see you have been trying to get back into the financial files." Doris jerked her head toward the computer. Edna looked back at Doris. "I understand now why my financials look such a fright."

Doris acted as if she was going to jump out of her chair and leave. Mike strode over and put one hand on her shoulder and in the other hand had the thumb drive. "You might want to put this in and turn the screen toward, Doris." Edna trusted that whatever Mike had up his sleeve was going to be good. "Mrs. Chessmore has not seen this yet, so it will surprise her too," said Mike.

Edna had the video up and running and turned the screen so Doris could see herself. It was amazing that the more it played, the madder Doris became at getting caught doing absolutely nothing. After several minutes, Edna shut it off.

"I want you to pack up your personal belongings and turn in your keys, work badge, and garage pass. Mike will assist you out of the building."

"It's illegal to video someone without their permission. I'll sue you."

"I didn't video you, Mike did. You can sue him. I knew I was going to let you go today. I just didn't know how bad your work ethic was until he showed it to us. You will get your vacation time, and I'll even be nice enough to pay you for the rest of this pay period, but I think you have dipped into my funds long enough."

Doris jumped up and stormed out of the office. She threw the door open so hard, it hit the wall. Mike followed and watched as she packed up her things. Doris was trying to throw some papers in her bag when Mike stopped her.

"Just personal items. If we find anything of yours later, we will make sure to get it to you."

Doris threw her keys and badge on the desk, stomped to the elevator, and Mike followed her to her car, which made her livid. He asked for the garage access card, and she threw it at him. He walked over to the attendant and handed it in before going back up to the office.

While Mike was gone, Edna went around to the rest of the staff and talked to them about their ongoing time studies. The two who had shown their lazy side had scribbled out some duties they had completed, but all of them were keeping track like she asked.

"I will be visiting with you all next week. Is anyone interested in the secretary position? It seems Doris won't be back." One hand went up. "All right. I'll talk with you in the morning." She walked back to her office just as Mike arrived.

He stopped at the desk to see what papers Doris was going to take and brought them into the office with him. "Mrs. Chessmore, you should look at these. Doris was going to take them with her."

Edna took them and reviewed the information. She had suspected that Doris was involved in the financial mess, but the information in front of her showed that she had to be working with someone else.

"Call Jordan back in."
"I'm on it."

Jordan showed up a half hour later in his salesman clothes, but by then the rest of the staff was gone. She made sure to turn up the volume on the radio, and they discussed things quietly.

"Have you checked out my secretary, Doris?"
"Yes, nothing showed up, why?" Edna turned the

papers toward him.

"I fired her today and she was going to take these with her, but Mike stopped her."

He looked them over. "We have a problem. It looks like she works at the direction of someone else."

There were several notations on the edges from someone explaining where to change the figures. They all paused, and Edna waited for someone to say something. Jordan finally spoke up.

"I don't know if any of this is related to the people watching you. You have some embezzling going on, but now it looks like it extends out of the office to someone that probably isn't employed by you and was using Doris as the fall guy. She probably didn't get much out of it, and that's why I didn't see any changes in her wealth. She's in the same apartment, drives a five-year-old car and has had the same daily routine for a long time. You're going to need more help than Mike and I can give you."

"Who are you suggesting I call now?" Edna asked.
"The FBI."
"Oh my."

Mike sat down beside her. "We have no idea how this all got started or why, but we need more help. If we don't call them, you could end up hurt. We don't know what is going on, but we've both been in this business a long time. You have to trust us to know when we need the big guns called in."

Edna got up and looked out the window. She could see someone waiting below. She turned back. "You're right. I can't live like this just waiting for someone to sneak up on me. Call them in."

Jordan made the call, and it was another two hours before someone showed up. While they waited, Edna called home and let Sarah know she wouldn't be there until very late. Jordan waited in the lobby and brought the man up to see Edna.

"Mrs. Chessmore, this is Agent Tom Edwards from the FBI." They shook hands, and everyone found a seat. "Okay, Mrs. Chessmore, give me your synopsis of what has been going on."

She started with her husband dying and how she holed up for six months before finally getting back out of the house to work. Then she started to see issues in the financials, talked to the CPA, and realized she was being followed.

"So I hired both Jordan and Mike to keep me safe, and they've done a nice job so far." The men both relayed what they had done up until today, including the new security system at the house. "So today I had to fire my secretary because I was paying her to sit out there and do nothing. I had my IT guy go through and fix all of the profiles and locked everyone out of several programs. One of which, was my secretary, who has never had any aptitude to learn how to work the financial program . She suddenly, over the last few month, has been able to manipulate the financials. But not good enough for me not to notice. I think she finally figured out I knew something wasn't right, and her behavior toward me became condescending and angry. When I fired her, she tried to take these papers with her, but Mike stopped her. It shows where someone has been changing the numbers. I know that isn't her handwriting, so someone else is telling her what to change each month. After we looked them over, we called Jordan in. Then he ended up calling you."

Tom sat and mulled things over. He took notes as the trio talked. "So the house and grounds are alarmed, Mike is your bodyguard, and Jordan has been looking at your staff and tailing your tails?"

"Correct."

"Can you afford to keep Mike on for a while?"

Edna sighed. "Yes, I can. Can I afford not to?"

"Good point."

Mike looked over at Edna. "Not a problem."

Tom looked over at Jordan. "We'll take over the surveillance then."

Jordan sighed. "Thanks. I hate that part. Just have Mike call me if you need me, Mrs. Chessmore. I'll be close by." She smiled at him. Jordan left the three to make their own plan of action. "Okay, Mrs. Chessmore. Let's go over your usual schedule and what you plan to do next week."

Edna explained what time she usually left the house and arrived at work, when she left for other appointments, and how she had been handling her lunch hour.

"I'm too afraid to go down the street like I used to and get lunch or shop. What I need to do is go see all of my retirement centers. I have twelve of them in three states, and I haven't been there since George died. I was hoping Max and I could take a day trip to see a couple of them."

Mike and Tom both said at the same time, "Max?"

"A good friend of our family. Maxamillian Harrison.

He has been a good friend of ours for years, and we helped him through the death of his wife. He offered to help me out and actually got me to work on my first day back. I haven't called him for a couple of weeks because I've been so busy, and I was hoping all of this would be over with by now."

Tom glanced over at Mike occasionally while taking notes. "Here's the deal. You can't tell Max anything. Nothing. Nada. Understand? If you used to do things together, continue. Your life has to look normal to whoever is keeping an eye on you. You can talk about work in a general way, but nothing about any of this."

Edna kept nodding. "So if I call him for a day trip, that's fine?"

"Yes. Just let Mike know where you are headed, and he will continue to drive you. He can be your chauffer or whatever you want to call him, but under no circumstances are you to be alone in anyone else's car. We will supply you a car with a tracking device so we don't have to stay close. It will be a small limo and would be a great cover story for having a driver."

"I like that idea. What about you, Mike? Care to chauffer me around?"

"I would love to, Mrs. Chessmore, as long as I don't have to wear one of those goofy hats."

"Okay. That's settled. Set your schedule for the next week and make sure they are just day trips for now. We need to take over for Jordan and follow up on the connection between Doris and whoever is instructing her to manipulate your financial papers. I will start tonight by getting everyone in place. In the meantime, go home and stay there."

"How do I get in touch with you if I need you?"

"Both Mike and Jordan have my number." She nodded. "The day is almost gone. I'm so sorry to take so much time but we had to get things settled. Do you mind if I borrow Mike for a little bit?"

"No, you can stay in here. I need to walk. I promise I won't leave the floor."

Edna walked out into the office area and decided to look over Doris's desk. She riffled through some files but didn't find any other incriminating evidence of manipulation. She even checked the trash and also noticed the shredder was full. She looked at the cubicles set up for the rest of her staff, and could see that some of them had family pictures, and some just liked to collect small items. Then there were the two desks that were in complete disarray, and she made note of that so she could bring it up next week. She would need to get Janda moved to Doris's desk first thing in the morning and settle her in. It sounded like she had been spending a lot of time answering the phone already. Before she knew it, the men were ready to have her return to her office. Tom informed her that he made a few calls, and men were already on the way to watch the house and in front of the building.

"We'll get to the bottom of this."

Mike headed for home, and Edna tried to relax as he drove. She tried to keep her mind off everything, but she kept coming back to Doris's betrayal plus someone following her. They ate a light supper since it was so late, and then Edna went to the den and called Max.

"I've been so worried about you. I wanted to call, but I knew you would be busy all day, and then probably tired at night. I was hoping you would get a hold of me, or I was going to have to just show up at the office and drag you out of there."

"Max, quit fretting. The first week was exhausting, but I'm back into a routine again, and I'm trying not to bring work home."

"Good girl."

"Anyway, I wanted to know if you're free for a couple of days. I want to take a day trip or two and check in with some of my retirement centers. I'm sure it will be boring, but we could catch up in between on the long drive."

"Absolutely. Anything for you, sweetheart. What time do you want me to pick you up?"

"Here's the thing. If you could stop by the office midmorning, that would be great. I have to break in a new secretary in the morning, and then we can go. I thought we could do lunch somewhere and then stop by both of the local centers before coming home."

"I'd be happy to come along and flirt with the nurses while you work."

"Oh, Max. I can count on you to keep things interesting. You are shameless."

"I'll be there around ten to ten thirty."

"Perfect. See you then."

Mike and Edna arrived at the office in a brand-new, shiny limo. He said he would wait in the garage like a good driver and keep an eye on the car so it didn't get scratched. She headed up to the office, and Janda was waiting for her. Edna spent the next two hours going over the computer programs she needed to use and made sure Barry had her profile fixed to meet her needs. She told Janda to spend the next two days cleaning up the desk area and organizing files.

"If I have a meeting come up, just put it on my computer calendar. It comes across my phone so no matter where I am, I can keep track of things. Doris was supposed to set up a special board meeting, but that didn't happen. I don't see one on my calendar. We always meet at least quarterly for a financial meeting, and that is coming up. Figure out when we met last and go from there. All of the names are in the email group, so you can just mass email an invite out. We meet in the board room here on this floor. If you have any questions, send me a text. Call only if you truly believe it's an emergency, like the office building burning down."

By the time she got Janda squared away and assigned her projects to the other staff, Max showed up to whisk her away.

"Are you ready?"
"Just let me close up my office, Max."

He watched as she locked up the desk and shut off the computer and grabbed her purse. As an afterthought, she picked up the bag she used to haul paperwork in and stuffed a pen and notebook inside. Shutting off the radio and then closing the door, she was finally ready to go.

"Your chariot awaits, my dear."
"Yes, it does, but it isn't yours." On the way down the

elevator, Edna explained she had a driver now, and they would be using her car instead.

"When did you get a driver? You have always driven yourself."

"My car is in the shop for a while, so I hired a driver. I liked it so much I decided to keep him around. I don't have to deal with the traffic, and you and I can visit easily without any distractions. It will be great."

"If you say so, but we always take my car, and there is no reason we can't this time."

"I can't write off your car, Max, but I can write this off."

Max hesitated as they entered the garage until he saw the car they would be using and whistled. "Well then, I can see why you like the ride. Nice wheels."

"I think so."

Mike opened the back door for Edna, and Max took himself around to get in the other side. She previously gave her agenda to Mike so he could program the GPS. They left the garage, and Edna called the first place they would be visiting and let them know she would arrive after lunch. She directed Mike to go to a sandwich shop close to Wind Haven. Max gave her a hard time about always eating in sandwich shops instead of restaurants, but she told him she wasn't in the mood for anything heavy while working.

Mike opened the door for Edna to get out and then walked over to the café and opened the door. When he followed the couple in, Max scowled at him.

"What do you think you're doing?"
"Having lunch?"
Edna patted Max's arm and told him to hush. "Stop

it. You'll make a scene. There is no way that I'll have him sit out there in the car while we dine. I take care of my employees."

Max mumbled something under his when Mike sat a table away from the two, watching the doorway for trouble and his own back to the wall. As soon as Mike was done, he left the café and waited out by the car. He spied the tail down the street and hoped that the guy was starving. Edna always seemed to know where the best cafes were, and he enjoyed every meal he had when around her. When the couple came out of the café, he assisted Edna back in the car and drove to Wind Haven. A few blocks away, Edna called her next stop and let them know she would be stopping by later that afternoon.

After assisting Edna out of the car in front of the center, he told her he would wait outside and pointed to a bench under the trees. She knew he was keeping an eye on things for her and remained comfortable in his presence. The administrator, Madelyn Flannigan, arrived to greet them.
Max told Edna he would wander around for a while before finding his way to Madelyn's office. Madelyn had always been one of Edna's favorite administrators, and they got along well. The administrator had a list of wants, and next to it was a list of needs.

"I budgeted for several of the things on the needs list, but we're finding the repair bills could exceed the cost of new on some of these items."

"I can see that. You never know when something will suddenly go out of commission. Let's look at your current financials, shall we?"

Madelyn reached over and grabbed a copy of the printouts. "Since I knew you were coming, I printed these off. It's a copy of what the CPA sends me every month."

Edna looked them over and noted there were no discrepancies. She turned to the budget, and they discussed ways around an extra purchase or two. "It's a pretty tight budget. Staffing is appropriate, and your current expenditures are in line. You just need more money in the capital budget for replacement. I'll take this list back to the office, and when we go to the board meeting we'll have to see what we can do. You won't be the only one with problems, so that will have to be our focus, I'm afraid."

Madelyn took her on a quick tour, and Edna was pleased with the way the facility was kept neat and clean. They found Max flirting with the nurses while on their tour.

"Pick on someone your own age, Max."
"I try, but they think I'm an old codger."
"More likely they know you're an old flirt."

The staff laughed at their banter. Edna thanked everyone for their care of the clients, and the couple headed out the door. Mike was waiting by the open door of the car and assisted Edna inside. He nodded at Max and let him get in on his own once again. Mike headed down the road to their next stop at Prairie Haven. He knew where it was located because he had an aunt who stayed there the last two years of her life. Once again, he waited outside and kept an eye on the tailing car. Edna didn't have any different outcome at this stop, and she felt both administrators were taking care of their share of the business legitimately.

She instructed Mike to take them to supper at a steak house on the way home. Edna already put it on the agenda for the day, but she was really into her role being chauffeured around. Mike decided to play a little game with their decoy, and when he hit traffic, he managed to lose it by switching lanes several times and going around blocks and coming out on a different highway. Edna knew what he was doing, but Max complained to Edna that he was a lousy driver and didn't know how to drive in rush-hour traffic. She ignored him and changed the subject.

Mike arrived at the restaurant and pulled into a spot right in front. Max was never lucky about getting a prime spot there and said so. Mike opened the door and assisted Edna out and then opened the restaurant door for her. A teenager walked up about that time and asked for a light. Mike reached in his pocket and handed him some bills instead. *"Thanks, kid."* The kid walked away smiling. Holding a parking spot for someone was easy money.

Mike followed the couple to a table, and he chose one close by, yet far enough away he didn't have to listen to Max drone on and on about himself. Max complained again about Edna feeding the help, but Edna stuck to her guns and told him to mind his own business.

"That's probably why you can't keep your own help. You don't appreciate them like I do. I treat mine like family, not servants. Don't mention it again."

Edna knew for a fact that Max had difficulty keeping staff. She could see why. He could be downright condescending and petty. All Mike knew was that he was going to appreciate a big steak tonight. The service was great and the food excellent. He left a generous tip even though he knew Edna would. He finished his drink and nodded to Edna as he left for the car.

During supper, Max asked about her secretary. "How come you had to break in a new secretary this morning? What happened to Doris?"

"Let's just say that doing some actual work was not on her agenda."

"Ah. Doris turned into a lazy Susan."

Edna chuckled. "Something like that."

"That's too bad. She's been there a long time and knows so much about your business." Edna nodded as she continued to eat her tender steak. "Do you think you'll give her a second chance? She's a nice girl."

"Why do you care so much?"

"No reason. I just know you depended on her for a long time. I would just think maybe a probation period would do her some good, then you could put her back to work."

Edna just shook her head. "It's too late for that. She turned everything in, and I have her out of the system."

Max looked perturbed. "It just seems like such a waste of talent." Edna finally put her fork down and looked at Max. He looked back and said, "What?"

"Since when do you care so much about my help? First, Mike, now Doris. What's up with that?"

He shrugged and picked up his own fork, ready to stop the conversation. Edna got the hint and finished her meal. On the way back to the office, Edna asked Max if he wanted to go visiting with her again in the morning, and he agreed.

"I'll call Brook Haven first thing in the morning and tell them we'll be there midmorning. We'll need to leave a little earlier since they are a couple hours from here."

"I'll pick you up around seven thirty."

"No, I will be driving right by your house. You'll come with me."

"But Edna..."

"Don't 'but' me, Max. If you want to go, you come in my car."

"You mean your limo."

"That's right."

Max could see by the look on her face there wasn't going to be a drive anywhere if he insisted on using his car, so he backed off. "I'll see you first thing in the morning then."

Mike parked behind the BMW and waited for Max to get out on his own. Max groaned, leaned over, and kissed Edna on the cheek. He then opened the door to get out. He almost slammed it shut but decided not to test Edna's temper. Mike pulled away into traffic, and headed for home. Edna checked her emails and text messages and noted that Janda added the new board meeting to the schedule and no crisis happened. She smiled and thought she would have to review the video footage to see how she was doing without her.

Edna's household all had an early breakfast and Max and Edna headed out to pick up Max. It was going to be a long travel day, and she and Max visited about friends and reminisced about functions they attended over the years.

The trip to the facilities was uneventful, and Edna was pleased with the visits. The staff laughed easily, and Max flirted unmercifully with anyone who could stand still long enough for his stories. Even some of the women who lived there enjoyed listening to him butter them up.

It was fairly quiet on the way back until Max brought up that he thought Edna should consider retiring. "I can see how tired you are. Have you given any more thought to selling out and retiring?"

"Not really. What would I do with myself every day?"

"It's great fun not to have all those responsibilities. I come and go, travel, whatever I feel like doing for the day."

They discussed the pros and cons until she tired of the subject. She finally agreed to think about it, though. More to shut Max up than anything. She watched the traffic out her window, and her mind wandered to the current problems. She was surprised when they pulled up to Max's house.

"I'll call you soon, Edna."

"Thanks for coming with me the last couple of days. It was good to catch up."

"Anytime. Next time, I drive."

Mike pulled the limo out to take Edna home. "You want to stop for supper? It's getting late."

"No, Sarah will have left something to warm up, and I want to get out of these shoes."

They sat quietly in the kitchen eating leftovers, and Edna contemplated Max's concern about retirement. "Maybe I should retire."

"I don't think you should make any decisions until all of this other mess is cleared up. If any of it is business related, just because you sell doesn't mean it goes away."

"How's that?"

"Just a gut feeling I have, and my gut is usually right."

"Well, I don't know what I want anymore. I have been conflicted about life in general since George died."

Mike's alarm went off on his phone. He pulled it out to look and scrambled to his rooms with Edna right behind him. He opened his laptop and logged on to the office cameras. There, just as bold as could be, was Doris riffling through the files and desk drawers. He called 911 and told them there was an intruder at the Chessmore Industries office building and Mrs. Chessmore was on the way.

They headed to the car and straight toward the office. He didn't even watch for a tail but knew that the FBI would be watching. He hit his stride with the traffic, and called Tom Edwards to tell him what was going on. Tom agreed to meet them there. He then handed his phone to Edna and told her which app to tap on and get the camera up and running so she could watch it while they drove.

The phone was harder to manage than the laptop, but she finally got it focused on Doris. She was making a mess of her old desk, flinging papers all over. Then she headed into Edna's office and was trying to get in her desk when the office security showed up. She tried to flirt her way out of trouble as she edged her way to the elevators. Then the police showed up and Doris was boxed in.

On the way to the office, he kicked himself for not

permanently disabling the floor button every night. He wanted to make sure employees always had access, but he knew someone would eventually turn it in to maintenance if they found the button not working. Doris was just being led away in handcuffs when Edna arrived. Doris scowled at her before being placed in the back of the cruiser. Mike led Edna over to the doorway, and she introduced herself to the officer manning the door.

"I'm Mrs. Edna Chessmore. Who do I need to talk to?"

"Go on up to your floor, Mrs. Chessmore. They are waiting for you there."

When they arrived, they found a team of men taking pictures and dusting for prints. Tom had beaten them to the office and led them to her office to stay out of the way.

"The locals are pretty curious as to why I'm involved, but I told them I'm just here as a courtesy to you at this point."

An officer walked into her office and interrupted. "Mrs. Chessmore I presume? Detective Johnson. Tell me about the intruder and how you knew she was here."

"I fired her a few days ago. She was my private secretary for a couple of years. I have security cameras installed in various places and it triggered an alarm at my house to notify me someone was here. That's when we called it in."

"Why did you let her go?"

"Mainly because she was being lazy and sloppy. She wasn't even answering the phones anymore."

"I see."

"She was deactivated from everything, but I assume she must have kept a spare key to get in the building."

"Will you be pressing charges?"

Edna looked around. "Yes, I don't know how else she will learn from her actions if I don't. She didn't look like she was too sorry when I saw her downstairs."

"Come to the office in the morning and make a statement. The men have finished up with everything, so you can straighten up now. Let us know if anything is missing, but we didn't find anything on her but her cell phone and purse."

Edna sighed as she and Mike started picking up papers and stacking them on the desk. "Janda is going to have a fit that all her hard work has been messed up. Doris used to be such a hard worker. I just don't know what happened to her."

Mike stood by and waited to see if anything was missing. "I will check with Tom and see if someone will review her personal phone calls. Even with a warrant, they have trouble with some of the phone companies. If she won't talk about who she is working for or let him look at the phone, he'll keep digging. Maybe a few days in jail will cool her heels a bit and she'll finally talk."

Edna left Janda a note to apologize for the mess, but explained there had been a break in and she had tried to straighten some of it up before they left. Mike brought Edna home, and she went straight to her bedroom. Mike cleaned up the kitchen before he turned in. He sat looking at the monitor and ran through the office video for the day. He would let Edna know in the morning that Janda was actually working and earning her keep.

Edna sat on the side of her bed and broke down crying. It started out as just a few tears, but then he couldn't stop. It all came pouring out for the months she spent grieving over George, her loneliness, the strange financial records, being followed, having to live with a bodyguard, a new alarm system, and work. Life seemed like such a burden now instead of joy. She cried and cried until there were finally no tears left. She curled up on the bed fully clothed, pulled the comforter over her, and fell into an exhausted sleep. The floor was covered with used tissues, and the light was still on.

Martha waited until the house was quiet before checking on her boss. It had become a habit of hers several months ago, and even though Edna started to get back to her normal routine, Martha continued to keep a close eye on her. She peeked into the room and saw all the tissues by the bedside. She sneaked into the room and cleaned everything up, then shut off the light. *"Poor Mrs. Chessmore."* She shook her head as she shut the door softly and went to her own room.

******

Edna took one last look in the mirror and was appalled at her puffy eyes. She took a hot shower and carefully applied her makeup. Once downstairs, she grabbed a cup of coffee and headed directly for the rose garden. She stood among the magnificent blooms and slowly inhaled the mixing fragrances. She continued to walk the grounds slowly and noted that the grounds keeper had brought her lawn back to its glory. He trimmed up the trees in the back, and the old leaves and broken branches were cleaned up.

All the while, she felt Mike keeping an eye on her. She felt secure but not infringed upon. It surprised her that she wasn't angry about him watching. Edna surmised that the crying was cathartic, and it was long overdue. She wandered back toward the house with no sign of Mike anywhere. She found him sitting at the counter having breakfast like he'd been there the whole time.

"You better eat something before we leave."

She nodded and took a plate from Sarah. "Pancakes this morning. Wonderful."

She ate in silence as Mike left the kitchen to get ready to go to the office. When he returned, Edna was sitting there enjoying another cup of coffee.

"I was wondering. Do you think you could set my den up as an office space? I'm tired of dealing with people following me. I'm comfortable here, and I could have Janda come to my house instead. I can send the rest of my staff to the other locations to work, and I wouldn't even have to supervise them anymore."

"Are you asking for an opinion or giving me orders to do something?"

Edna thought about it for a moment. "Just an opinion, right now."

"It would be easy to change locations to your home. Your IT guy can transfer everything here. Lord knows the den is big enough. So you're thinking of closing the office then?"

"Yes. I'm a sitting duck there. Between that garage and me being on the top floor, I'm pinned in eight hours a day. It would be easier to watch them outside my house and not have to deal with traffic. I can wander the grounds at will and actually consider this a trial time to see if I want to retire or not."

"When we get to the office, we'll call Tom in and see what he thinks." She nodded and finished her coffee. "But we need to stop at the police station to give your statement first."

Edna groaned. Janda proved to be a great asset and had everything put away by the time Edna arrived. "Mrs. Chessmore. I'm so sorry. Did they take anything?"

"No. The person got caught in the middle of trashing the place. Thank you for taking care of this mess so quickly."

"No problem. Anything special you would like me to do today?"

"Maybe later. I'll let you know. I'll be expecting a visitor soon, one of the men that was here the other day. Bring him right in when he arrives."

"Will do."

Tom arrived midmorning to find Edna staring out the window. Mike arrived shortly before him and was sitting in a corner leafing through a magazine. Tom walked over to the window and looked out.

She pointed to the sidewalk across the street. "Someone is always there. Always. Then if I leave, they're at the house. What are they waiting for?"

"I don't know. Yet."

"I suppose you have no grounds for an arrest."

"No. And if I did, whoever the boss is just calls in someone else just like when the locals arrested all those people with the stolen plates. No one talks, and they walk. The men pay a fine, and they are back to work. As long as they prove themselves to their boss, they have a well-paying job."

Edna turned and walked to her desk. "See this mess? I can't get anything done. I worry about coming and going. I worry about someone running me off the road. I worry about being shot in the garage or the building blowing up. I can't live under these conditions. Now I have this cute, young secretary ready to prove herself, and I can't even focus enough to teach her anything. I spent six months holed up in my bedroom so depressed I couldn't function after George died. Now that I'm finally among the living, I'm still a prisoner." She pointed at Tom. "You. You need to fix this." She flopped into her chair and stared at Tom.

"Of course. You're right. But I've only had the case less than a week. You need to get away from here for a couple of weeks where no one can follow you. I can get you out of town. You and Mike, that is. Is there somewhere you can go?"

"I need to go see all of my retirement centers out of state. I usually fly."

"You will have to drive this time. I'll get you a different car, and you can leave the limo in the driveway. We will make sure you aren't followed, and you will leave after dark. Get enough cash to get you by for a couple of weeks. No trace of a credit card or checks. No flights. Tell your secretary you are away on a personal emergency and call her on a throwaway phone. Mike will make sure you change phones frequently. Go conduct your business and move around frequently. Enjoy the sights. That will give us a little more time to hunt down the person causing this entire problem. I might even be able to break Doris into telling us who is behind her embezzlement scam. I'll get someone similar to Mike to stay at the house and come and go as usual. They'll never catch on. They aren't the brightest bunch on the planet. Someone will do something, and we'll catch them. Hopefully, someone will give us the whole story."

"I need the freedom to walk around without looking over my shoulder."

"Just let me know when."

Edna looked around. "Friday night will be fine. I can let Janda know I have to leave town, and she will be in charge while I'm gone."

Tom turned to Mike. "Keep in touch. We'll plan on Friday night then." He tipped his hat and headed out the door with Mike following. When they got to the garage, they worked out the details to get Edna out of town.

"Who do you think is behind all of this?" Mike asked.

"I have no idea right now, but we are always suspicious of certain people. Why they would want to follow Edna is the mystery."

"Do you think Doris is connected to this other stuff?"

"We have no idea right now. It just seems too coincidental to not have some relationship to the case. Does Mrs. Chessmore have any suspects?" Tom asked.

"After the Doris episode, she believes she is somehow involved, but other than that she hasn't mentioned anyone else."

"We managed to get Doris's phone records. Nothing in them. Unless she has a throwaway phone she used on the side. We are waiting to search her apartment. I've convinced the judge to not allow bail for the time being. I also have someone trying to check her bank records."

They finished up, and Mike headed back upstairs. He walked into Edna's office and said, "Mrs. Chessmore?"

"Mike?" He shut the door. "Get a brand-new laptop

and have your IT guy set it up for you."

Edna didn't even ask why. She called Barry and arranged a time for him to stop by. Then she got online and ordered a laptop and portable printer to be delivered immediately. "Done. Now what do I need to spend money on? I keep this up, and I'll be broke by the end of the year."

Mike cringed. "Sorry, Mrs. Chessmore. Maybe we can recover some of this after the FBI figures it all out. Speaking of money, you need to get some cash. Do you have a local branch close by?"

Edna groaned. "This is ridiculous. Utterly ridiculous." She paused. "Two blocks down on the right."

"Let's walk."

"Walk?"

"Yeah. Freak out the bad guys. You walk, and I'll walk behind the tail. No one will touch you."

"Wow. Fresh air in the middle of the day."

"You go in and get some cash, tuck it way down in your bra before you leave the bank. If someone thinks you have cash, they'll try for your purse. I'll use the ATM outside the bank and get my own cash."

"I'll just take my wallet. I have a lot of things in my bag for work, so I won't need it. Let's go."

Edna told Janda she was expecting a new laptop and to just set it on her desk when it arrived. If Barry arrived before her, he was to program it so she could use it while away from the office. Edna planned on going to lunch while out too, so she explained she wasn't sure what time she would be back.

Edna crossed the street right in front of the watcher, and she smiled at him before heading down the street. He followed at a discreet distance while talking on the phone. He was so distracted; he didn't realize Mike was on his heels listening to the call. Edna went on into the bank without incident.

Mike stopped at the ATM and withdrew some cash while keeping an eye on the man. Edna came back out and beamed at the man before heading across the street to her favorite café. Just as the man started to follow, Mike "accidently" ran into him and knocked him down, the man's phone flying. Mike ended up lying on top of the man and apologized profusely.

"I'm sorry. I didn't see you there. Hang on a minute, son, while I get up."

Someone walked by and picked up the phone. Mike reached out to take it and rolled off the man in one swoop. He pocketed the phone and reached out to help the smaller man on his feet. "You okay, man?"

"Yeah. You knocked the air out of me though."

"Sorry, man. I was in a hurry."

He left the guy dusting himself off and looking for the phone. Mike tore across the street, entered the café, and found Edna at her favorite table.

"What did you do to that kid?"

"I ran over him." Mike pulled out his own phone and sent a quick text to Tom. "Let's order."

Edna glanced out the window and noted the kid was panicking. She smiled and ordered her favorite meal. Just as lunch arrived, so did Tom. He took a plastic bag out of his pocket, and Mike put a phone into it. Tom nodded and left, and Mike went back to eating.

"Kid's phone?"
"Yip."

The rest of the day flew by with Edna preparing for her trip away. She double-timed all the paperwork, and had a whole list of things for Janda to do while she was out of the office. Edna walked out to the staff and asked to look at their time studies.

"I'm sorry, I haven't gotten back to these the last couple of days. Write your name on them and hand them to me as I stop by your desk. I promise to get back to you as soon as I return." Edna walked around and visited quietly with each employee and thanked them for the jobs they did.

When Edna finally sat relaxing on her couch with a cup of tea in her hands, she thought about packing a bag but just couldn't do it. There was always tomorrow. She told Martha and Sarah at supper that she would be out of town for several days to get away from all of the stress. They totally understood and encouraged her to have a good time. Due to the people following her, Edna reminded them to go about their business as usual and not change their schedule. They were to pretend she was holed up in the house.

Edna picked up her cell phone and called Max. "I have a heavy schedule the next couple of weeks, so you probably won't be hearing from me."

"Anything I can do for you? Need a companion?"

"Thanks, Max, but no. I just need to take care of some personal business, and once I get through the next couple of weeks I can decide if I want to retire or not."

"I hope you decide it's time to hand it over to someone else. It is just such a large company, and without George, I worry about you."

"I appreciate it, Max, even though that's a sexist remark about a woman's ability to run a company."

"That's not what I meant, Edna. You know that."

"I just wanted you to know why I won't be calling or being available for calls. I promise I'll call you once the dust settles."

Edna hung up the phone and finished her tea while feeling quite melancholy. Max hung up and was confused at why Edna would be too busy to call.

Friday afternoon, Edna was anxious to leave work. She spent the last couple of days working with Janda and felt her new secretary was catching on very quickly.

"I need to be gone for several days on personal business. I'll call to check in and help answer questions if I have the time. Just email me at the end of every day and let me know what is going on. I can answer any questions when I read them. If there is a crisis at one of the other corporations, tell them to handle it. They did a nice job while I was out of the office, and they don't need my approval." Janda kept nodding and paying attention. "Doris was let go because she wasn't doing anything around here anymore."

"I know. We all knew that. She drove us crazy bossing us around and not doing her own job. I'm surprised any of us stayed while you were out of the office."

"I appreciate your loyalty. All of you. You won't let me down, will you?"

"No, ma'am. The rest of us want to keep our jobs, and as far as I know, everyone gets their work done on time."

"That's good to know, Janda. You're in charge while I'm gone." Janda became a nervous wreck and began to wring her hands. Edna chuckled. "You'll be fine. Enjoy your weekend."

Edna gathered up her new laptop and a few files, locked her desk, and then closed her office door. She waved at Janda and the rest of the staff as the elevator doors closed. She sent a text to Mike, and he was in the garage ready to take her home.

Mike stood by the car waiting for Edna. After several minutes, he walked into the building. The front receptionist was already gone for the day, and there was little foot traffic. The elevator dinged, and he watched the doors open. No Edna. He pulled out his phone and called Tom.

"Do you still have an eye on the place?"
"Yes, why?"
"Mrs. Chessmore didn't show up to the car. I'm headed upstairs." He hung up the phone and caught the next elevator, hoping he didn't miss her coming down. When he arrived at the office, Janda was just leaving.

"Mrs. Chessmore left several minutes ago. I thought she was meeting you in the garage?"

"I must have made a mistake. I'll head back down. Thanks."

Mike went into full panic mode. He took the stairs instead of the elevator and headed down full bore. By the time he got to the lobby, Tom was there with his men.

"We've got someone looking at the security cameras. We didn't miss her by much."

"Where was your guy? I thought he was watching?"

"Yeah, well, he and I will be having a conversation shortly." Tom nodded toward a young man who was pacing the lobby.

Mike stormed over to the young man. "What were you doing that was so important you couldn't do your job?"

The man swallowed, blushed, and stammered. "I had to go to the bathroom. Bad. I wasn't gone that long."

"Long enough to lose the client, you moron."

Mike stomped back to Tom's side and waited for the security videos to be looked at. A few minutes later, the agent came running and yelled, "I got it." He gave the information to other agents, and they took off. The agent explained to Tom and Mike that the video showed someone pulling Edna toward a waiting car, and shoved her in. Then the man ran to the driver's side, got in, and drove off. The plate was visible, and the picture of the man was sent over to Tom's office for facial recognition. Tom took off with the rest of the men and left Mike standing in the dust. He finally shook himself and headed for the car about the same time as Janda came through the lobby.

"Did you find her?"
"She caught another ride. I'm headed back home."
"Oh. All right. Good night."

Mike rushed back to the house, and for a lack of anything else to do, he reviewed the footage of the office and then of the house and grounds. There was nothing there. Knowing it wouldn't do any good to call Tom, he did text Jordan. Now he had to tell the staff. Supper would be just about ready, so Mike headed for the kitchen. He asked the women to sit down. They knew by the look on his face something was up. They quit chattering and promptly sat in their chairs.

"We think Mrs. Chessmore was kidnapped this afternoon."

They shrieked, moaned, and cried. Once they began to calm down, Mike explained that when she didn't show up at the car, he went looking for her. All he could tell them was the FBI was on the case and he hoped that they could catch up quickly. He tried to reassure the women, but he wondered who was going to reassure him.

In the meantime, the FBI hightailed it after the car, and the local police were called in to assist. There were a few traffic cameras around the city, and the car was seen briefly, only to lose it rapidly. It was as if the driver knew exactly where all the cameras were. The plate number was stolen—again. No one ever talked when they were arrested, and phones were always throwaway and were already disconnected by the time the officers looked at them. The car disappeared from their radar and everything came to a standstill.

PART TWO

Edna felt terrible. Something smelled terrible. Her head hurt, and her mouth felt severely dry like she hadn't had a drink of water in days. She tried to lick her lips and couldn't because something was over her mouth. She tried to open her eyes to see where she was, and it was pitch black. Edna, always one to remain calm in the middle of a storm, began to panic. She assessed herself and realized she was lying on something hard, her hands and feet bound. Lying there trying to calm herself, she regulated her breathing and began to listen to the surrounding sounds but only heard muffled noises in the distance. The sweet, sickly smell was coming from her gag, and it made her want to vomit. She took a few more slow breaths through her nose, and it seemed to help the nausea, but it also made her drowsy. She felt herself losing consciousness and tried to fight the feeling. It was a lost cause.

Edna's kidnapper sat watching TV and having a beer. His favorite baseball team was playing, and he was happy to have nothing to do except kick back and watch the game. He was getting a tidy sum for handling the job, and he planned to make the best of it. The setup was perfect for him. The guy who hired him would be by later that evening and would let him know what he needed to do next. All he cared about right now was the game and his beer.

A few hours later, the boss walked in and found the man asleep in front of the TV with a scattered twelve pack of empty beer cans around him. The boss looked around and attempted to locate Edna. Shutting the TV off, he listened for any sounds. Worried, he kicked the man's leg. Jerking awake, the man sat up and yelled out at the same time. The boss scowled at the other man.

"Where is Mrs. Chessmore?"
"Where? Here."
"You better hope so because I can't see her."
"I've got her tucked away in a closet in the other room."
"Closet? What do you mean in the closet?"
"I didn't want her yelling and making noises. I decided the closet was a good place to stick her."
"Has she got a blanket or a mattress?"
"No, why should she? You wanted me to kidnap someone. You didn't say you wanted me to babysit. I thought she was your prisoner? You don't make prisoners comfortable."
The boss looked at him. "So you're telling me when you spent time on the inside you didn't get a mattress?"
"Well, yeah, I did."
The boss groaned. "Let her out of the closet and give her the bed. She's a fine, high-class woman and doesn't deserve to be treated like a dog."

The man grumbled and went to the other room, weaving as he went. He managed to get the closet open and dragged her out by pulling under her arms. Edna awakened enough to feel the movement and groaned.

"Bathroom," she mumbled through her gag.
"What?"
"Pee. I have to pee."
"Just great." He was about to tell her to pee her pants when he saw the boss looking at him.

"Take her bindings off and walk her to the bathroom."

The man tried to protest, but the look on his boss's face stopped him cold. He whipped out a switchblade and cut through the bindings quickly and helped Edna up to the bathroom. She had difficulty walking since she was so stiff and sore from lying on the floor tied up.

"Leave your gag and blindfold on."

He shut the door and waited for her. When she finished up, he walked her back to the bed and pushed her, causing Edna to fall back. She yelped as she fell but was grateful it was a soft bed she landed on.

"Stay there. I'll be right back. Someone is in the room watching, so don't try anything."

Edna believed him. She heard someone talking, but the voices were none she recognized. The man was soon back and applied new bindings to her feet and hands. He told her to get comfortable and stay put. The man threw a blanket over her and left the room, shutting off the lights behind him. She heard the lock click, and the tears rolled down her cheeks, soaking her blindfold first. Edna eventually cried herself back to sleep.

The boss and his employee talked quietly in the front room. It was past midnight, and both of them were tired. "I'll be back tomorrow evening. Take care of her like she was your own grandmother. Unbind her in the morning but keep her locked in that room. Have her wear the blindfold anytime you open the door to bring her food or take her to the bathroom. Otherwise, leave her alone and don't touch her. I better not see any mistreatment when I return."

The man shrugged and kicked back to sleep in the recliner. He wasn't happy to have to give up the bed, but the man did as he was told. He took all of Edna's bindings off the following morning. He brought her some donuts and juice from the kitchen and helped himself to eggs and bacon. He was bored stiff with nothing but daytime TV and no beer, but for every hour he took care of the lady, the more money he made. He dug out a deck of cards and spent part of the day playing solitaire until he finally found a game on TV to watch.

Edna spent most of the day pacing in the room. She could leave the blindfold off until she needed to go to the bathroom or the man would bring her something to eat. The windows were covered with shutters on the outside, and she had no idea what time of day it was. That morning, she could smell bacon frying, but he only fed her donuts and they were disgustingly dry. She had to depend on her mealtimes to know what time it was. The man was a terrible cook, but she wasn't that hungry anyway. She certainly wasn't going to complain because she remembered how quickly he had sliced off her bindings the night before and knew he must carry a sharp knife of some kind.

She gradually walked the headache off. The smelly stuff on her gag had definitely been more than she could stand, and even after it was removed the smell remained on her skin. Once in the bathroom, she tried to wash her face and get some of it off, but the smell must have been in her sinuses. She shivered thinking about the possibility she could be dead instead. She was waiting for the other shoe to drop, and she paced harder just thinking about what could happen to her at any time.

******

After a restless night, Mike looked at the video of the front gate and saw someone sitting there. *"What the heck?"* He sent a text to Tom and asked if he had an agent watching the house. He replied *"No."* Mike puzzled over it while having coffee with the staff and realized he'd seen the car before. The women were sullen, and Sarah put out cold cereal instead of cooking.

Mike looked at the women. "I'll be back. I want to check on something."

Mike left in the limo and drove to the office like usual and parked in the garage even though it was Saturday. He got out and waited in the shadows before taking the elevator up to Edna's floor. He had free rein of the place since no one was in the office. He walked over to Edna's window and looked down. Sure enough, someone was standing there, keeping an eye on the place. He left and came back a couple of hours later, and the man was still there. He waited awhile before leaving, and the man followed him back to the house.

Mike stood at the monitors and watched. He sent a text to Jordan to stop by when he was free and see if the person out front was someone he was familiar with. In the meantime, Mike visited with Martha and Sarah and told them to continue their normal errands and duties because the house was still being watched.

Jordan stopped by the front gate, and Mike let him in. Once in the house, they discussed that the same men were still watching the house and office just as if Edna was still around. It was puzzling, and they finally called Tom and put him on speakerphone so they could all talk about the situation. Tom was just as surprised as they were to find them still being watched and decided he needed to get an agent back out on their trail.

"The only thing I can figure out is that they aren't the ones she left with. Someone else must have taken her. Just keep up the appearance like she is there and make sure the alarm system is working."

Jordan promised to check with some of his sources on the street to see what they heard, and Mike promised to pretend to drive Edna back and forth to work.

******

The boss returned that evening to check on Edna and was pleased to see her without a blemish. The boss paid the man with an envelope of bills and told him to disappear.

"I've heard the FBI identified your face from the security cameras. You better leave town."

The man grinned when he looked in the envelope and left the house without looking back. He hadn't had a beer all day and would find the first bar he could on the outskirts of town.

The boss knocked on the bedroom door. "Put your blindfold on." He waited briefly before hearing an acknowledgment. He unlocked the door and shut off the lights, leaving the glow of the living room light behind him. "We're going for a drive. Do you need to use the bathroom first?"

"No. I went a little bit ago."

"All right. Let's go. Keep the blindfold on at all times. I won't bind you as long as you don't try anything."

He led her to the car in the garage, shutting the lights off as he went. Once he had her in the back seat, he put the seatbelt on her followed by snapping a hard bracelet to her wrist.

As they pulled onto the road, he told Edna, "The back doors have a child safety lock so you won't be able to open the doors. I have no plans to harm you in any way. I'm taking you to safety, but I can't let you know where it is."

Edna tried to figure out the sounds of the city, but there was nothing that stood out. She didn't ask any questions and tried to figure out why she would be kidnapped and then told she was being taken to safety. It wasn't long before she realized they left the city and were on the highway headed away to parts unknown. Somewhere along the way, the man put on some soft music, and Edna felt herself drift off.

It wasn't until the car slowed down and hit a rough road that Edna was jostled awake again, while the car slowly wound itself on a dirt road. She could hear the tires change sound as he turned one last time onto crushed rock and stopped.

The driver got out and helped her with the seatbelt, activated the bracelet, and assisted her out of the car while holding her by the elbow. He carefully led her up some steps and opened the door to a cabin, turned on the lights, and left her standing inside the doorway while he remained outside in the shadows.

"Stay facing that direction while you listen to me. I am going to leave you here, and when you can't hear the car any longer, you can take the blindfold off. There is no way to walk out of here because you are miles from civilization. There is no cell service or landlines. I left your laptop and purse inside the door. It will do you no good here, but I wanted you to know I didn't steal it. You will have satellite TV and a fully-stocked kitchen and pantry. The bracelet will only come off when I'm ready to take it off. It will alert you to the electronic perimeter, and it will give you just a light tapping when you start getting too close. If you continue into the electronic field, the shock will become stronger until it gives you a jolt like a stun gun. The place is covered in video feed and microphones. I don't have cameras in the bathrooms and bedrooms, just mikes. They aren't there just to keep an eye on you, but to make sure no one bothers you or attempts to harm you. I will come back in about a week to bring more groceries, but you don't come out to meet me. I will drop them off, and you can pick things up after I'm gone. Please take the time to relax and enjoy yourself. Think of it as a vacation, and remember you are safe here. One more thing—you can call me James." With that, he shut the door and left.

James watched the video feed of the cabin from his place in the city in between his other activities, and at the end of the week he took another load of fresh fruit and vegetables to the cabin. It was dark when he arrived. He put the groceries by the door and left. He knew she would wait until he was gone before opening the door. Glancing in the rear view mirror, he had almost lost sight of the cabin before she opened the door to pick up the groceries.

Edna spent the week resting, watching old movies on TV, and walking the beautiful mountainside as far as she could go. She had to test the bracelet and found that she didn't like the shock it would emit if she walked too far. Edna made a mental note as to how far she could wander in all directions. Thankfully, it was a large area, and she was definitely enjoying the sunshine. She found herself talking out loud to keep herself company.

As the days turned into a week, she was surprised at how little she was worried about her company or herself. Edna hoped that James was serious and that he was protecting her, but she had no choice but to try to make the best of the situation. She thought about Mike and how he was probably going nuts looking for her. Then there was the FBI and Jordan. All that help and she was still taken from under their noses. Edna chuckled at the irony of the situation.

******

Mike made his usual drive in the limo to the office and back every day, and in his own car, he followed Martha and Sarah the first few days to make sure no one was bothering them. He felt reassured the tail only followed the limo. He and Jordan scheduled a visit to the jail to visit Doris. Tom made a deal with the judge to hold her without bond, and the hearing kept getting delayed. Doris had been cooling her heels a long time, and they hoped by now she was ready to talk.

Mike and Jordan walked into a room where Doris was already sitting and waiting. She didn't seem very happy to see them, Mike smiled and Doris scowled back.

"What do you guys want with me?"
The men sat down across from her and looked at Doris until she became uncomfortable. "I see sitting in a jail cell hasn't made you any friendlier."
"Look. You're the one who had that video of me without my permission and got me fired. I don't have to be nice to you."
"So it's my fault you're sitting in here?"
"That's right." Doris crossed her arms, sat back, and glared at Mike.
"Let's see. So far, they have you on criminal mischief and breaking and entering. All minor stuff, yet you were denied bail. Interesting. I would say that's because of the embezzling charge that is pending."
Doris sat up. "Embezzling? What are you talking about?"
"When you manipulate numbers to take someone else's money from their company, they call that embezzling.

That will cost you about twenty years behind bars if I'm not mistaken. Is that about right, Jordan?" Mike looked over at him. Jordan nodded.

"I didn't take any money."

"That's not what the paperwork proves. It's got your name all over it, and we just came by to ask you what you did with all that money."

"I didn't take it. I don't know what you're talking about."

"Okay. Whatever you say. Just thought we could help you out, but you must love it in here. Come on, man. We're out of here."

They got up to leave, and as they reached the door, Doris yelled out, "Wait." They stopped and turned. "I didn't take the money. Someone else did."

The men came back to the table. "Spill."

Doris sighed, knowing she was beaten at her own game. "I was contacted by phone several months ago by someone, and he said he could help me pay my bills if I would help him get a few bucks occasionally. I was behind on my rent and car payment, so I thought it sounded like easy money. Once I figured out how to take a few bucks here and there, the person caught up all my bills. About that time, Mr. Chessmore died, and Mrs. Chessmore never came to the office. That's when I got calls about taking more and more money each month and putting it in a special account. I didn't get anything out of it except my car is paid off and the rent was paid for a year."

"Who is it?"

"I never saw the man. The money was put into a corporate account at the First National Bank. I wrote a check every month for the account, and then I tried to hide the payment. It was a weird name. Spelled JINX."

"How much is gone?"

"I lost track. Thousands?"

"Like ten thousand or a hundred thousand?"

Doris thought for a moment to calculate the figure. "It was over several months. Probably more than a hundred thousand. It started out with smaller amounts, and then it escalated to over ten thousand every time I transferred the money. Even I could tell the company wasn't going to sustain that kind of loss."

"Why did you keep doing it?"

"Someone threatened me to continue to take the money or else they would make sure I wouldn't see the light of day again."

"And you have no idea who it is?"

"Never saw the guy. The calls were always made from a café or a gas station, so I never had his personal number. The other thing about the threats, the voice was different than the one that I gave the money to."

Mike looked over at Jordan. He had been quiet the whole time and shrugged at Mike. "We'll look into it."

They left Doris sitting there wondering if telling all she knew would make any difference in her sentencing.

******

James had been watching Edna's house for weeks and got the pattern down for what was going on. The tail was still there, and whoever was driving the limo continued to go to the office and back every day just like Edna was home. That was working out well for him in the scheme of things. Real well.

The two women left to do their weekly shopping, and

he followed. Parking beside them in the parking lot of the grocers, he got his own cart and picked up a couple of canned items. He stopped to ask them where the bread was, and Martha told him which aisle it was on. James came up behind them in line and stood there.

Martha turned around, and he smiled. "Go on ahead of us, young man. You don't have near the load we have."

"Thank you." James pushed his cart in front of them and paid for his groceries. He stood at the end of the counter, placing the change in his wallet while the women chatted with the clerk. He turned to the ladies and said, "I can see you have a lot of bags today. You were so nice to me, I'll help you load the car."

"You don't have to do that. We're used to handling our own groceries."

"I insist. I'm in no hurry." He waited patiently for them and carried his own bag while pushing their cart out to their car.

"This way, young man." They led him to their car and popped open the trunk.

"I'm parked right beside you." They all laughed at the coincidence.

James loaded the trunk with their groceries and said goodbye. "Drive carefully now."

James put his own bag in the back and walked over to his door. At the same time, the women realized their car wouldn't start. Martha opened the door. "Deader than a mackerel. I don't know what's wrong with it. I'll have to call a service truck."

"Ladies, you have all that food. Let me take you home and then you can get the truck called later. There's no sense in having your food go to waste in this heat."

"Are you sure it won't be a bother?"

"No, ma'am. No bother at all. Let's get those groceries transferred, and we'll get on the road."

Martha and Sarah got out and helped change the groceries from one car to the other. James conveniently had a cooler to put the meat in. He assisted both women into the back seat of the car and got in to drive. They gave him the directions, and as he pulled out of the parking lot, he asked if it would be all right if he made a quick stop first since it would be on the way. They agreed without question. He pulled into an out-of-the-way shopping mall, parked close by the front door of a clothing store, shut off the engine, and turned in his seat to face the women.

"Ladies, here's the deal. I need you to go into the store and buy some clothes. A lot of them." He paused, and the women looked at him like he had grown two heads. "I'll come with you and pay for it, but this is the deal. Would you like to see Mrs. Chessmore?"

The women were shocked. "What?" they said at the same time.

"Mrs. Chessmore is safe and sound tucked away, but she has no clothes with her. I'm taking you to her, but you will all need clothes. Do you think you could do that?" They both nodded their heads but sat there in shock.

James got them out of the car and led them into the store. They immediately bought several outfits for themselves and Edna. The cart was brimming with items when James brought over another cart and asked them to get Edna some tennis shoes and make sure they all had underwear. If it hadn't been such a stressful situation, the women would have had a good time shopping. James pulled out a disposable Visa card and paid for everything. The car was loaded completely full between the groceries and the clothes. He made sure the women were settled between their packages, then handed them each a blindfold.

"Put them on after we leave the parking lot. You can't know where we are going since it's for your own safety." He then put a bracelet on each person and shut the door. He pulled out of the parking lot and into the busy street. "Now, women, let me explain everything. First of all, my name is James." They dutifully put their blindfolds on as he explained about the bracelets and why he couldn't let them see where they were going. "After this is all over, I don't want anyone to know where you have been. It's a safe house, and there is only one other person that is aware of the place. I won't hurt you and Mrs. Chessmore. My plan is to actually keep you all safe from harm. The best way you can do that is to keep each other company and enjoy your vacation. Just follow the rules, and we'll be fine."

When they were done asking questions, James turned on some soft music. Martha and Sarah held each other's hands for the whole trip. When James pulled into the drive of the cabin, he didn't get too close as it was still light. He was wearing a disguise; and with his dark glasses, hat, and scruffy beard, he doubted anyone would recognize the real man behind it. He opened the back and took all the groceries out first, followed by the mountain of clothing. James opened one back door and activated the bracelets. He then assisted the women out of the car and told them to wait until he left the driveway before they started for the cabin.

"I'll return another day. You three should have plenty of groceries to last a long time."

James left, and the women took their blindfolds off and began to yell for Mrs. Chessmore. Edna heard a car, but she had dutifully stayed in the house. When she heard the car drive off, she was shocked to hear women calling her name. She threw open the door and ran down the steps and met Martha and Sarah halfway from the cabin. They all talked at once and cried at seeing each other again. Edna was thrilled there was a change of clothes, and it took two trips for all the packages to get taken into the cabin. While they were working on unpacking the groceries, the women explained how they were picked up at the store and brought to her.

"It was a man named James."
"Yes. That's the name of the guy that brought me here, too. What did he look like?"
"Oh, a hat, beard, dark glasses. Nice looking. I guess we were so worked up over everything that we didn't really look that close, but it's no one we've seen before. He was a perfect gentleman, though."

Edna showed the women around the cabin, and they took all of their clothes to their rooms. Edna proclaimed a shower was in store now that she had clean clothes to put on. She was thrilled with the tennis shoes as her hard-soled shoes from work were awful to walk in outside in the rough terrain. Sarah headed for the kitchen and set to work preparing a meal, doing what she did best.

******

Mike saw the women leave early that afternoon for their usual grocery run. A message was sent to Tom about the conversation with Doris, and he was waiting for a callback. As the afternoon waned, he began to become worried and called Martha. When she didn't pick up, he called Sarah. Still no answer. The phones both went directly to voicemail, and it instantly made him question what happened. He called Jordan to come over, and they both went searching for the women.

Mike drove straight to the grocers, and the car was still in the parking lot. He went into the store while Jordan checked on the car. The women left hours ago, and the store had no security cameras installed. By the time Mike got back to the car, Jordan found the problem. The battery was completely unhooked, and now it looked like someone had taken the women.

"For a bodyguard, I'm doing a lousy job."

Jordan called Tom, and they agreed to take the car back to the house. With no security video, there was nothing to track at the store, so he would send someone over to dust the car for fingerprints once they got it back to the house. Jordan always wore gloves, so he drove the car. Someone in his line of work was used to never leaving prints behind. By the time they got the car home, an agent was waiting for them.

Mike had had enough. "I'm going to move ahead to plan B."

Jordan was watching the agent dust for prints.

"What's that? Plan B? I didn't know we even had a plan A at this point."

"If I had done what Mrs. Chessmore wanted to do in the first place, she'd be safe."

"What?"

"Move her office to the house. Those yahoos think she still goes back and forth to work anyway, so I might as well save the effort on my part."

"If you can pull that off without her being here, more power to ya'."

"A lot of help you turned out to be."

"I don't do hard labor. If you need anything else, I'm your man." With that, Jordan took off.

When the agent completed his job, Mike left in the limo to supposedly pick up Edna once again. The following day, once he made his obligatory stop at the office, he headed to the other two offices to follow up on Edna's plan to farm out her staff. He found them more than willing to take on staff who wouldn't increase their payroll, but would increase their productivity. They each had room for half of the staff, and Mike would arrange to have them moved lock, stock, and barrel the following week. He then went back to the main office to talk to Janda. He asked her into Mrs. Chessmore's office and closed the door. He explained the plan to have the corporate office moved to the house and the rest split up and moved to the other two offices.

She was surprised but professional about the move.

Janda agreed to call Barry and ask him to get everything coordinated with the IT department, and she found a number that Mrs. Chessmore used for moving furniture and supplies. Once everything was arranged, Mike went out to let the staff know what would be happening the following week.

"I know this is sudden, but as you know Mrs. Chessmore is on leave again for a personal emergency. In her stead, I'm going forward with her decision to close down this office and move you to one of the other offices. If you have a preference, let Janda know. If it doesn't matter, then you will go where there is a slot open. Your jobs are all secure, and Mrs. Chessmore appreciates everything you do. This has been a tough year for her, and she is trying to make it easier for everyone involved. IT will be setting up your workstations next week. You can all take Monday off with pay while the movers take your belongings to the new office. You will then start at your new office on Tuesday, and Barry and his team will get you all set up. Take your personal belongings home with you and just leave work-related items behind. Lock all of the filing cabinets and secure the desks when you leave tonight. Mrs. Chessmore's and Janda's desks will be taken elsewhere. Does anyone have any questions that I can answer?"

A hand went up. "What if we don't want to move?"

"Then I guess you're out of a job because this floor will be vacated as of Monday. Like I said, if you have a preference on which office you move to, let Janda know. Each desk will be marked with the name of the office because they will be loaded on separate trucks."

Mike waited as the staff talked among themselves. When no one else seemed to have any questions, he went back to Janda. "One last thing. Let the board know that the office is closing and that the board meeting will be held at the house. You will have to cater the meal in. Are you up to all of this?"

"I guess I have to be, don't I?"

Mike smiled. "Mrs. Chessmore was right. She knew you could do the job."

He left his personal number with her and told her she needed to be in the office on Monday to direct the movers. He would plan on seeing her at the house later on Monday, and Barry planned to personally take care of the server and have her up and running by the end of the day. He also gave Janda the access code to the gate so she could come and go. Now if everything else could go as smoothly and they could find Mrs. Chessmore, he hoped that she wouldn't mind him closing down the office.

******

The board gathered at Edna's house on schedule, and Mike agreed to make sure the caterers could set up in the kitchen and had everything they needed. He felt they could have the meeting sitting at the dining room table. He watched Janda meet everyone at the door upon their arrival and brought each one to the dining room.

The group poured themselves drinks from the wet bar that Mike set up for that purpose. He wasn't sure how much of the house Edna would usually use for guests and tried to keep them to just a couple of rooms. Since there wasn't anyone to clean up afterwards, he would be responsible for any spills or accidents, and he wasn't really into household work.

The six board members arrived, along with the two managers from the Chessmore Group, followed by Carson Shoemaker. Mike pulled Carson aside and introduced himself as a friend of Jordan's, and explained that the funds were actually removed by Doris. But they still had no idea who received them. Mike didn't want to have anyone aware of the embezzlement as of yet. Carson understood and stated he brought only what was expected, not the adjusted books Doris made. Carson designated the missing funds as owner draw off until they could explain where it went. Mike nodded in agreement as Janda started to get everyone's attention.

She nervously stood to the side and asked everyone to have a seat. Dinner would be served, and then they would get right to the board meeting. That was Mike's cue to notify the caterers it was time to serve dinner. He told Janda earlier he would eat in the kitchen so the board wouldn't ask any questions as to why he was there. He was also going to be first on the agenda in a closed session of the meeting and wanted to make sure everything else went smoothly up to that point.

Mike picked at his meal, much to the consternation of the caterers. He reassured them he was just nervous because of the meeting and if they would leave him some leftovers, he would sure appreciate it. The crew did their job and worked at cleaning up efficiently as they went along.

By the time dessert was served, the kitchen was almost spotless. The dishwasher was running, and the catering van was practically packed. He thanked them profusely, and as promised, they left a large amount of leftovers in the refrigerator. As they gathered up the dessert dishes, which were fancy plastic, they disposed of the garbage and took the bags out to the dumpster. They waved goodbye, and Mike breathed a sigh of relief when they left. So far so good.

Mike stood in the background and barely listened to the meeting. He didn't really want to know about Chessmore Industries anyway, but he did want to know who was on the board. Jordan popped in right after the caterers left and helped himself to some food before joining Mike in watching the proceedings. He invited Jordan to get a feel for the board members and how they reacted to Mike when he talked. Carson discussed the financials, and the other managers brought their needs to the board as previously asked by Mrs. Chessmore.

The managers were disappointed she wasn't there because they wanted to thank her for allowing the repairs and new equipment to happen earlier than the new budget year. Carson reassured the board that the financials were strong enough to sustain some unexpected expenses and the increased productivity would help recover the cost. Once the managers were done with their reports, they and Carson left for the night. It wasn't long before Janda was letting the board know she needed to make the next part of the meeting a closed session to discuss employee issues. Now it was Mike's turn to face the board.

Mike walked in and introduced himself. "I know that I do not have any authority in this room, but we need to discuss Mrs. Chessmore. As you know, she took Mr. Chessmore's death pretty hard and did not leave the house for about six months. In that time, the board took care of their normal business and did it well. Mr. Shoemaker attested Chessmore Industries is doing well financially. On that note, Mrs. Chessmore has suddenly been needed elsewhere on personal business. She knows it is a terrible time to leave but has had no choice. She is asking that someone be designated as a temporary CEO while she is gone. She feels that the company will run smoother knowing they all have someone to turn to for issues like equipment failures."

Occasional murmurs occurred while he talked turned into loud discussions. One of the men on the board stood up. "Quiet now. So you are asking that one of the board members be designated as temporary CEO?"

"Yes, sir."

The man looked around at everyone. "I'll do it if no one else objects."

The group sat discussing the pros and cons of each person in the room, and the man sat down beside Janda and asked her several questions to which Janda had few answers.

Mike finally tapped on the table to get their attention. "I'm stepping out of the room now. I've delivered all the information I have. Thank you."

Mike went to stand by Jordan in the shadows of the dark kitchen. Jordan pointed to the man that first stood up. They watched in silence. The man stood up again.

"I say. Are we ready to decide yet?"

"Bradley, sit down, you pompous fool." One of the women scowled at him and stood up. "As Bradley has forgotten, this is a temporary measure to make sure we have a captain for the ship, not a bloody takeover. I've known Edna for over thirty years. Our kids went to school together. She doesn't need someone coming in to take over anything, just a go-to person when a crisis arises. I say we write down who we want on a piece of paper and have Janda read the results. Then we can move this meeting along."

Everyone agreed except Bradley. Janda quickly made up small pieces of paper and handed them around. She reached over to a bowl on the wet bar, and as they voted, the papers were put in the bowl. Janda went back to her seat and counted them out loud.

"Mrs. Whethers, you have the deciding votes. I call this meeting back into regular session."

The board made the vote a part of the regular meeting to make it legal, and Janda asked Mrs. Whethers to continue the rest of the meeting as acting CEO. Mike and Jordan looked on as Mrs. Whethers conducted the meeting flawlessly the rest of the evening, with Bradley moping throughout the night. Before Jordan left, he told Mike he would check into the board members, especially good ole' Bradley.

Tom called Mike the following day and told him that the bank account Doris used to deposit the large checks in was closed and it would take a special subpoena to get the name of the holder. Doris was still locked up, awaiting her arraignment. She never once asked for bail according to Tom, which meant she was truly scared of someone outside the jail. Mike looked at the video, and the tail was gone. While on the phone with Tom, he asked about it, and he said his agents hadn't seen one out there since late evening. If no one showed up in the next day or two, he would call his guys off and use them in some other way on the case.

Janda showed up like clockwork every day and conducted business appropriately. Mike didn't want to leave her by herself in the Chessmores' big house, so he continued to stay in the guest rooms. He got in the habit of stopping by his own apartment every few days to get the mail and water his plants. He stayed out of Janda's way, but made sure she had free rein of the kitchen. She eventually began to feel comfortable in her surroundings and made herself at home. The two of them sat down to lunch and were enjoying a cup of coffee when Janda made an observation.

"It's too bad Mrs. Chessmore isn't here what with this big old house and no one in here but us."

"I know. Hopefully, she will be home soon. Would you like to move in for a while? There is a whole other set of suites on the other side of the house and you wouldn't have to make the drive every day."

"No thanks. I have a great apartment, and it isn't that far from here actually. I don't think it would look right if I moved in, first of all, and I would hate to lose my apartment."

Mike grinned. "I understand. I'm overstepping my bounds making the invitation anyway. I'm just kinda' stuck here by myself and could use some company occasionally. I probably just need to get out more."

"I never did know what your title or job is for Mrs. Chessmore. I don't have you on the payroll."

"That's a good question. First of all, she pays me privately. I was hired to be her driver and manage her security. She didn't have any type of alarm system, and we've set up a state-of-the-art network for her. I continue to monitor her security for her, but since she's gone, there isn't much to monitor."

"Oh. That makes sense. Well, I better get back to work."

Mike sat finishing his coffee and wondered why he was still hanging around. He had let Edna down, and now she was gone. Although he could send a monthly bill to Carson Shoemaker to pay him for his time, he felt like he didn't earn it. It was definitely a conundrum.

Mrs. Whethers came to the house once a week to check with Janda and signed paperwork and checks. Mike stayed out of the room but could hear them talking. Nothing seemed to be out of the ordinary, and after business was conducted Mrs. Whethers promptly left.

Jordan did background checks on Mrs. Whethers and other board members and found nothing to be alarmed about, but the verdict was still out on Bradley Jenkins. Jordan was still working on that one. With the weekend coming up and no need to be at the house, Mike packed up his duffle bag, locked up the house tight, set all the alarms on his way out, and went home to his apartment until Monday morning.

******

The house was dark, and the man looked out his window into the black night. There was no moon or stars to be seen due to the heavy cloud cover. The city glittered below him, and the cars looked like ants scurrying back and forth. Located high on a hill surrounded on three sides by trees and rocks, the only way in was driving up a long, curving private road. No one could arrive unannounced.

Gregory Marchman was not a happy man. The last few years his heart had become as black as the night in front of him. If asked, he couldn't say when he had let evil overtake his actions as it gradually became a part of life. The more wealth he accumulated, the more he wanted. And when he wanted something, he took it. Until now. The wheels were in motion, but then they suddenly came to a screeching halt when Edna Chessmore disappeared.

The people he hired were always someone he considered expendable. If they were caught and didn't talk, he paid them to go away and stay away. With veiled threats about what would happen if anyone talked, he hadn't had to worry about what he would do next. Everyone had a price, and his underlings always did as they were told, no questions asked.

He also knew someone was watching and waiting for him to make the next move. He just didn't know who it was or why. Anytime someone accumulated unexpected and unexplained wealth as quickly as Gregory Marchman, it always put you on the radar from multiple entities.

Waiting for the latest report, he finally spotted a vehicle coming up the drive. He hoped for the right answer this time. Gregory met the man in the front of the house. He spent time with pleasantries, and he wasn't about to start tonight. The meeting was short, and he stomped back into the house, slamming the door behind him. The car left in a hurry, hoping to get away from the anger as quickly as possible.

******

The women spent all their time visiting and wandering the area. Edna finally made them call her by her first name, and after about a week Martha and Sarah finally became comfortable doing so.

"After all, if we're going to be stuck here together, we might as well act like the friends we are."

The women took that as a compliment and began to enjoy the relaxation the cabin offered. Martha stumbled across a closet that held multiple card and board games, and they spent the evenings trying to best each other. Sarah began teaching Edna a few simple dishes, but she found desserts more to her liking. Both making and eating.

The women eventually came across some berry bushes and couldn't wait until they were ripe enough to make a pie. Sarah exclaimed that if the bears didn't beat her to them, she would have enough to make jelly. The women got in the habit of tacking a note for grocery or personal needs on the door for James to take when he stopped by, and Sarah added canning supplies to their next list.

Shortly after their arrival, Martha and Sarah both thought they should contact their families and asked James to mail letters for them. The women wrote they were on an unexpected trip with their boss and would be gone an indefinite amount of time and would let them know when they returned. James told them he would honor their wishes and took the letters to mail.

Although both Martha and Sarah could talk to and see James, Edna was never allowed the privilege. They all assumed she would recognize the man, but his voice never gave him away. After a couple of weeks, they did ask him how long they would be kept there, and all he could say was that it would be an indeterminate amount of time until he could assure Edna's safety. The women all agreed that if they were truly safe, they would be happy to spend the summer in the mountains.

******

James spent a few hours every week working as the gardener at the Chessmore residence. He proved his worth to his boss who had more than enough requests to keep him busy. He agreed to take on only one place and mentioned that the Chessmore property would keep him busy enough for the summer. The foreman worked the property long enough to know how much work it could be and was happy for someone else to take it on. Martha happily gave the gate code to the owner of the company, and James had free rein in and out of the gate now.

James pulled in on a Saturday morning and drove around to the back as he usually did. He already knew where all the cameras were. He walked directly to the garden shed to get the pruning shears. The rose garden needed work, and he wasn't going to let it get out of control. He had seen the mess earlier in the season, and when Mrs. Chessmore pruned the plot, it was with loving hands. James went to work before the sun rose too high in the sky to spend time in the heat. He completed his task and took the loaded wheelbarrow to the compost pile. He then went to work on the yard.

As he completed the mowing, he parked by the back door and rang the bell. He was sure no one was there, but thought he would ring the bell anyway. When no one answered, he used the code to go into the house. He continued to have his garden gloves on and left them in place. James didn't know for sure if there were cameras in the house, but he assumed there were.

He carefully made his way to the kitchen and got a glass of water. After downing the first one, he got a second, wiped the rim off with his glove, and put the glass in the dishwasher. He left the same way he came in, reset the alarm, and took the mower to the shed before leaving for the day. He smiled as he made his plan to return that evening after dark. James arrived back on that dark Saturday night and let himself in the house. He stood quietly listening for any signs of life. When he was assured he was by himself, he walked directly to the den and fiddled with the security equipment until he got all the house cameras off. Then he turned on a small desk light and began searching for the information he needed.

The den had changed since he was in there last, and he realized that the business office was now located in the house. He missed that changeover but had wondered why there wasn't any activity at the office downtown. He found what he was looking for, and took down the painting to find the wall safe still intact. He carefully used the combination numbers, and after two tries he was able to successfully open the door.

Looking through a variety of papers, he finally pulled out exactly what he needed. He replaced everything back in order and closed the safe tight, spun the dial, and hung the painting back over it. James shut off the light, put the cameras back on, and left the house, resetting the alarm system without leaving a trace.

******

Jordan spent several days tracking Bradley Jenkins, and the more he tracked, the more he didn't like what he saw. He met Tom in a coffee shop right outside Jenkins's office, and they visited about what Jordan found. When he completed the outline of events, Tom sat staring across the street.

"Maybe we finally got a break. I owe you big time if this pans out," Tom said.
"You owe me big time from the last time I helped you. I'm still waiting to get paid for that one." Jordan said.
"I'll buy the coffee this time."
"Great. Don't forget the tip." Jordan got up and left the shop.

Tom sat and watched Jenkins's office, and then decided to make a visit. His receptionist said he was in a corporate meeting and would be tied up most of the day. Tom refused to leave a name and said he would be back. After leaving the office, he called his most trusted agent and began the formal process of investigating Mr. Jenkins.

******

When Edna had been gone over three weeks, Maxamillian began to call the office and home numbers. He left so many messages on the home phone, it finally filled up the voicemail. He hounded Janda to tell him where Mrs. Chessmore was, but Janda could no more tell him than Mike could. One day, he arrived at the gate and demanded to be let in. Mike was there and buzzed the man through. Janda had no desire to see him as he had left a sour taste in her mouth from the phone conversations.

"Just let him rant and rave. I've met the man, and he's all bluff and blunder. I'll be outside the door if he gets too belligerent," Mike said. Janda felt better knowing Mike would be there.

Max came charging into the house, and when he saw the den door open, he flew in and stopped in his tracks. The den had been completely made over to the office, and he saw Janda sitting behind her desk.

"May I help you?"
"Who are you and why are you here? What is going on?"
Janda remained sitting to control her shaky knees. "My name is Janda, and I'm Mrs. Chessmore's secretary."
"What are you doing here?"

"I work here."

Max groaned. "Why is the office here? I went by the tower, and the floor is closed down."

"Sir, what is your name?"

Max stopped ranting long enough to be appalled that Janda didn't know him. He stood tall and threw back his shoulders. "I am Maxamillian Harrison, and Mrs. Chessmore is one of my dearest friends. I demand to know what is going on."

"Sir, the office was moved here shortly after she left on an extended vacation. If she didn't tell you anything about it, then I can't help you."

"You, Missy, are impertinent. Don't you be snubbing your nose at me."

Mike heard enough and walked into the room. "I believe you have thrown your weight around long enough. It is duly noted that you are miffed that Mrs. Chessmore hasn't kept you informed, but her secretary is doing her job and doing it well. I believe that if Mrs. Chessmore wants you to know anything else, she will contact you."

Max became angrier as Mike talked. "You don't speak to me that way either. As soon I get a hold of Edna, I will encourage her to fire both of you."

"I believe that Mrs. Chessmore made it very clear that her staff is her business, and she abhors the way you treat your own staff. Don't presume to believe you have any influence over her decisions. Now, if you will please leave, Janda needs to get back to work. Let me escort you to the door."

"I can find my own way out. Believe me. You haven't heard the last out of me." Max turned and stormed out of the house.

Janda breathed a sigh of relief. "He's really mad."

"All talk. He **won't** bother you again. Next time, we won't let him in the gate."

They both laughed, which helped Janda's nerves. She calmed down and went back to work. Out of anything better to do, Mike reviewed the security tapes for the house and noted the entrance of the gardener. He watched for a while and decided the man was doing an excellent job but didn't know why he had the access code. Mike assumed Martha or Sarah had given it to him.

He shut off the feed and went out to the rose garden. The automatic drip watering system kept the roses properly wet, and they had bloomed off and on all season. He had gotten used to going out in the morning as Edna taught him, and started the day walking his way through the roses, teaching himself the names of each one. He stood looking around. *"This must be what retirement looks like. I just might consider it myself."*

******

Gregory Marchman sent his man away with a new mission—get the information he needed no matter what it took. Without Edna Chessmore, he needed to take other measures because time had run out. Waiting was never his strong suit, and his patience was already thin. He took one more look out the window for signs of someone arriving with good news for a change, but was disappointed once again. He decided to get a couple of hours of sleep, if possible, before dealing with any more problems. It looked like he might actually have to do this job himself.

The man sped from Marchman's place, smarting from the tongue lashing he was given. He stopped to pick up another man and headed directly to the Chessmore house. They were both quite familiar as the men had been part of the stakeout teams. How she managed to disappear out from under their noses, he didn't know. Word on the street was that the FBI didn't even know where she was. Everyone watched the office close down, and they only assumed she had been taken before then.

It was close to midnight when the men pulled up on the side street by the Chessmore house. Nothing stirred, and they got out of the car quietly. Scaling the fence was easy, and they kept in the shadows while approaching the house. They had seen the security truck and watched them set up the equipment. The alarm system was somewhere on the back of the house out of sight.

They carefully stuck to the shadows, then one of the men pointed up at a box that was higher than you could reach. The other man went to the gardening shed and pulled out a ladder, climbed up, and disarmed the wires. The men went to the back door and jimmied the lock to get in and successfully managed to open the door. They stood still to make sure there were no surprises such as dogs or someone waiting for them. When they didn't hear a sound, they continued into the house and finally found the den. One of the men turned on a table lamp, and they both took a side of the room and searched every nook and cranny available.

Just as one man lifted a painting off the wall to expose a wall safe, they heard the click of a gun hammer. The men both turned, one with a painting in his hands. Not armed, they knew they were both in trouble. Two very burly men stood there glaring at them, and both were armed. Mike and Jordan had come running when the first silent alarm sounded.

"Gentlemen, we'd advise you to lie flat on the floor." The men looked at each other, shrugged, and did as they were told. "While we're waiting for the police to show up, why not tell us what you were looking for?" Neither man spoke nor made a sound. Mike walked over and looked at the safe. "I assume it must have something to do with the safe. Do you have the combination on you?" The two men remained silent. Mike reached down and checked pockets but didn't find anything, including ID. "I guess we will just wait then."

A few minutes later, the police arrived and led the men away. Mike explained to the detective, after the men were out of the room, that the alarm box was a dummy, and all the silent alarms were tripped from the moment the men scaled the fence. He promised a copy of the tape of the men both outside and inside the house, and would drop it off in the morning. Since they were stopped and nothing was taken, their sentencing would be light. Like everyone before, he assumed no one would talk, but it must have something to do with the safe. Not that he would ever be able to get into it to find out.

Once the police were gone, Mike hung the painting back in place and straightened the room. He and Jordan worked on fixing the back door so it would lock and then

Mike took Jordan home and stopped at his apartment to get a couple of hours of sleep.

Once he was rested, Mike went to the Chessmore house to run a copy of the video for the police. He decided, since he was looking at it, he would preview from where he left off previously. As usual, he was fast-forwarding the tape when he noticed a quick blip. He stopped the tape and rewound it part way. He watched it in real time, noticed a quick shadow, then noted the time stamp. The next time he noticed any movement, the time stamp showed ten minutes later.

Mike brought up the rest of the cameras and set it to the appropriate time frames. He noticed a shadow in and out of the house, using the code on the door. The shadow moved directly to the den and went to the camera control box. The next thing he knew, the cameras were filming again and the shadow moved back out of the house. The car that the person was using was out of range, so he had no idea what the person was driving. Something happened in those ten minutes, and it was before the other men had broken in and found the safe. He called Tom.

While waiting for Tom to show up, Mike changed the codes to the gate and security system. He would have to be there before Janda on Monday to let her in, and he decided not to let anyone know what the codes were until Mrs. Chessmore returned. Tom arrived, and Mike showed him the strange video, plus gave him a copy of the whole evening.

"I gave a copy to the police of the men they arrested, but they don't know about someone showing up before that. I didn't realize it until I started to preview it to make their copy," Mike said.

"Thanks for the video," Tom said. "I'll see if my guys can get anything else from it. We are on to something. I don't know if it will pan out as far as finding Mrs. Chessmore, but it's a start. We'll know more tomorrow."

"I hope you find her soon. We evidently had two different sets of break-ins overnight, and I'm betting they both have something to do with the safe."

"That does seem a little too obvious, doesn't it? I'll get back to you when I know something. By the way, Doris is still sitting in jail. She refuses bond and says she will do her time and get it over with."

"So did the judge give her a break because she gave us information?"

"Not on the office trashing. The embezzlement charges are on hold until we can complete our investigation. She seems content to stay where she is."

"Weird."

"I need to get home. My wife will kill me if I miss church again."

******

Tom and his agents spent the next couple of days finishing up their investigation into Bradley Jenkins's life and were finally ready to approach him. They walked into his office and asked his secretary to see him immediately, flashing their badges as they did so. The secretary jumped up and took them to Bradley's office and opened the door.

Bradley was on the phone, and he jumped up as the men came in and stood before him. The secretary quickly closed the door as Bradley ended his conversation abruptly and hung up the phone.

"What is the meaning of barging in here like this?"

Tom flipped open his badge and asked Bradley to sit down. He dropped into his chair. "We'd like to ask you a few questions, Mr. Jenkins, and we would certainly like some answers."

Bradley bit his bottom lip as he mulled over his next action. "Am I under arrest for something?" he asked innocently.

"Not yet. Are you willing to answer some questions?"

"Maybe."

"It's a yes-or-no question, Mr. Jenkins. Or maybe we should call you JINX?"

Bradley shrunk from the statement. "I better call my lawyer."

"For what reason, Mr. Jenkins?"

"I don't like this line of questioning."

"I haven't asked you anything in particular yet. So you are not willing to answer my questions?"

"No, I'm calling my lawyer."

"All righty then. Men, take him in."

Bradley reached for the phone, but the agents cuffed him first. "You can call him from my office."

They led Bradley out of the office, and he yelled at his secretary to call his lawyer and get him over to the FBI office immediately. She was picking up the phone as the men walked out to the car.

Bradley sat in an interrogation room waiting for his lawyer to arrive. It seemed like hours, but the man arrived forty minutes later. Mr. Popoff had been his lawyer for years, but he had never needed him more than he did now. Bradley explained that the FBI came to his office and knew about a bank account he had in a dummy corporation name. When Doris was arrested, his part in the extortion and embezzlement process came to an end, and he closed the account out immediately. The problem was, he was being threatened by someone else, and now things were looking bleak for him. Bradley needed to explain how he got mixed up with the wrong type of people when he was gambling, and now he owed thousands of dollars to a bookie.

Mr. Popoff sat there amazed at the story his old client was telling him.

"You are going to admit to everything. And I mean everything. Extortion is a crime in itself. In order to go after the men going after you, you will have to work with the FBI to sort this entire mess out. All I can do is represent you and hope we can get a lighter sentence. This is serious stuff. Now you have me involved to some extent. I can't support the mess you've made out of your life. You do it my way or you can find yourself someone else."

Bradley hoped his lawyer would tell him to stay quiet and let the system try to prove he was guilty, but to no avail. He knew he was right and would have to confess to everything. He nodded to Mr. Popoff, and the lawyer got up to let the FBI know his client was ready to talk. Tom and another agent came in and recorded the story that Bradley told them. They asked multiple questions over the course of the next hour, but Tom had one more.

"Tell me. Why is Doris afraid of you?"

Bradley puzzled over it for a moment. "I don't know. She shouldn't be because I never threatened her. I made calls and helped her take the money. She deposited it in my account, but I never contacted her except to get the money. I paid her rent for the year and paid off her car as compensation for getting the funds I needed to forward on to someone else."

"Do you think that your bookie was threatening her?"

"I have no idea. I didn't think anyone else knew where I was getting the money."

The agents worked with Mr. Popoff and Bradley to lay out a plan of action, and a new agent assigned to his case took him back to work. Bradley was to explain to his secretary it was all a mistake and that they released him once they figured out they had the wrong guy. His secretary had worked for Bradley for years and was relieved to see him return to work.

Bradley sat in his office chair behind closed doors the rest of the day, worrying about his future. He got up once and looked out the window to see the agent watching the office from across the street in the coffee shop. He wasn't sure it was a comfort or worrisome because he didn't know if the agent was watching him or watching out for him. Only time would tell.

PART THREE

Gregory Marchman managed to get a few hours of sleep without interruption. He would have preferred to be interrupted with the news of a successful mission, but he knew that wouldn't happen by the time he decided to turn in for the night which, in fact, was early morning. He sat in his sterile-looking kitchen with its stainless steel countertops, table, and appliances. The walls were white, and the chairs and floor were the only color allowed—black.

Drinking a cup of coffee and nibbling on a piece of toast, he read the morning paper as he did every day, but he never saw any news on Edna Chessmore having gone missing nor of a break-in from the previous night. It was as if she never existed. *"Why was it kept quiet? What is going on?"*

He finished his toast, poured himself another cup of coffee, and went back to the window overlooking the city. It was waking up, but it made Gregory's life feel insignificant from his point of view. He was raised in a typical American family. His parents, still alive, had remained married to each other, raised two children, and now had four grandchildren, none of which were his. His sister continued the tradition by marrying her college sweetheart and was very involved in her children's lives.

Holidays were always filled with laughter and love, but Gregory, always sullen, never felt as if he fit in. Even as a youngster, he would brood over the simplest things in life and tended to make sure someone else got the blame for his mistakes. His sister eventually got tired of his behavior and stayed away from him. She found her own circle of friends and, due to her sunny nature, had many of them. Gregory tended to be a loner, and even though his parents continually encouraged him, he never found his own niche in school.

Even when he went to college for a business degree, he never developed any lasting friendships.

Although his whole family went to church most Sundays, Gregory quit going as a teen and never went back. As time went on, he used his sullenness to drive his skill at making money, leading him down a darker path to get there. When he wanted something, no one would get in his way. No one. His parents were never impressed by his wealth, which irked him greatly. He offered to buy his family homes or cars, and they refused to take anything extravagant. One wedding anniversary he offered to buy his parents a cruise around the world, but they stated they just wanted to stay home and go out with friends. Even his family knew he had a black heart. Only his business associates appreciated his skill as an entrepreneur, but he knew they would never stand by him as friends if times got tough or he failed.

He finished his coffee, then readied himself to head into the city. He was tired of hiring fools to get the job done. It was time for him to find out what was going on and to take things in his own hands. Gregory sped into the city driving his black Lamborghini. He loved the feel of the power, and on his own long, curving access road, he drove it fast and hard. It was about the only time he ever smiled.

He pulled into the garage at his corporate headquarters and found his way to his reserved, overly large personal parking space protected by his own attendant. The car, when locked, had an alarm that would go off when something or someone was as close as three feet, and the attendant had a remote to reset it as needed. The attendant was paid well to make sure no one would park anywhere close to that area, even on busy days.

Gregory walked into his office in the penthouse overlooking the city. The whole floor was windows everywhere you looked. He figured if you're going to have a penthouse, you might as well see the underlings below you. Looking out over the city from the office, unlike at his home, he felt the strength of dominance. Gregory led his businesses with a power he developed when he began his career. Over time, he was surprised how fast his corporation grew. The penthouse was the only place he felt he really belonged.

In accordance with his nature, he found a secretary with similar behaviors, and she handled clients just as easily as he did. One look at her, and no one would think to argue when she said no to someone. Karen updated him on the day's appointments in her typical no-nonsense fashion and proceeded to get back to her own work.

While Gregory waited for his first appointment, he looked out across the city until he could pinpoint several of his own businesses. It was a game he played most mornings, seeking what was his as if to make sure it was real. "*Now if I can figure out how to clear up the latest mess.*"

His first appointment arrived, and Gregory began to get into the rhythm of the day. Bradley Jenkins was interested in selling his chain of optometry stores and was hoping to make a great deal with the Marchman Corporation. Bradley was so far in debt, he had to find a legitimate way to get out of trouble. His lawyer suggested selling out as a way to keep the value of his businesses before people found out he was in trouble for embezzling. Gregory smelled blood and knew he was going to get a great deal. When people try to sell off a successful business, he knew there was more to it than management just needing a change. He had his secretary do the groundwork on the operation before the meeting, and decided the corporation would be a great addition to his portfolio.

Bradley asked high, Marchman lowballed the offer, and they worked out a figure they were both happy with. Gregory figured he was much happier about the agreement, but whatever was going on with this Jenkins guy, it would probably get him out of the trouble he was in. The deal would definitely make his corporation more money. As his business day was wrapping up, he left the office, giving Karen a quick wave. She nodded as he walked out the door, and then picked up the phone to make a call. "He's on the way." She hung up and finished her work for the day.

Karen spent six years in Mr. Marchman's employ, and they never had a personal conversation since neither one cared about each other's personal life. Karen was paid extremely well to make sure Mr. Marchman's office ran smoothly. She picked up her purse and keys to leave, looked around, and wondered how long it would last. Something was happening and she absolutely wanted no part of whatever it was.

Gregory found a parking spot several spaces away from everyone else and hoped, when he returned, his car would still be scratch free. He set the alarm and headed into the building to hold what he hoped to be a solution to his problem. Shaking hands with the man, Gregory was offered a drink before sitting down. He declined and hoped the next fifteen minutes would prove fruitful. Instead, an hour later, he slammed out of the office, leaving a completely nervous man inside.

When he sped out of the garage and headed for home, he found himself stuck in traffic instead. Turning off at the next intersection, he drove until he found a park, pulled in and came to a screeching stop. Walking around in his business suit would cause people to look, but he had to solve problems and he wasn't going to do it stuck in traffic. He threw his jacket and tie in the car, rolled up his shirt sleeves, and walked over to the pond to watch the swans gracefully float by. He didn't know how long he stood there, but he was no closer to solving anything as when he arrived. Pulling out his phone, he made one last call for the day and arranged a meeting for later that evening. Satisfied, he headed to his favorite restaurant for supper while waiting for the men to arrive. He ate so much at this particular place that the manager automatically saved his table from five until eight each evening just in case he showed up. No matter how busy they were, Gregory always had a table waiting and a place reserved in the employee parking lot for his car.

He was just finishing his meal and enjoying a glass of wine when the three attorneys showed up and were escorted directly his table. Bruce Hansen, Steve Perry, and Mark Lincoln, all partners in an attorney's office, were summoned to see Gregory Marchman. When you were summoned, you came. They couldn't afford not to since they were all in too deep. They ordered their drinks and made small talk while waiting to be served.

"Gentleman. Have you located the papers?" They all shook their heads. "So what are we going to do? I sent someone to retrieve them the other night, but it seems the place is like Fort Knox." The men all tried to blame each other for the mess they were in. "Stop it." Gregory hissed.

The men all settled down. "What about her friend, oh, what's his name? Does he know where Edna is?"

Bruce spoke up. "Maxamillian. I'll talk to him. We go to the same clubs. My wife and Edna were good friends too. We might be able to use ole' Max. I have it on good authority he is just waiting until a year is up, and then he's going after Edna to marry him. He's running through his money like water and needs a refill. In the meantime, he's hanging out with any rich widow he can find in case something better comes along." The other men nodded as Bruce spoke.

"Interesting," Gregory said. "So he has his own scam going. He could be useful to us. You work on that and get back to me. Steve? Mark? You men have any other ideas?"

They both shook their heads, but Steve finally spoke up. "I'll go visit Edna's secretary and see if she can help us find the missing file." Everyone agreed Steve could charm a snake to give him what he wanted.

Gregory puzzled the problem. "If Edna found it, maybe that's why she disappeared. And why doesn't anyone know where she is? Word on the street is that the FBI doesn't even know where she is. Why isn't it spread all over the news she is missing?" Gregory finished his drink and stared at the men, making them more uncomfortable. "If someone else finds it and realizes what we've done, we're all in trouble. All of us. There is no fall guy."

The men all got up and walked away, knowing time was of the essence. Bruce headed straight for the clubs in search of Max. It took three different parking lots before he found the distinctive BMW he was looking for. He stopped in and found Max hanging out with three widows, all dripping in diamonds.

"Max, buddy. How are ya'?" Bruce slapped him on the shoulder as he spoke.

"Good, you?"

"Great. How about we go to the bar and I'll buy you a drink?"

"Sounds great. Ladies, I'll be back later."

The men visited briefly before Bruce asked about Edna. "My wife asked how she was doing, and I had to admit I haven't seen her in months."

"Last time I saw her, she was working full steam ahead. I was trying to convince her to sell out and retire, but she wasn't having anything to do with that idea. She just got back to work after George died, so I thought I'd give it a break for a while and try to get her to retire later after she'd worked for a few months. She called me a few of weeks ago and said she'd be out of town for a couple of weeks, but after three weeks I went to the office to see her and the office was closed down. I went to the house, and everything from the office is moved over to her den. I tried to get some information from her snippy secretary, but she and Edna's chauffer practically kicked me out. I tell you what, when Edna gets back, I'm going to tell her to fire them both."

Bruce continued to nod as Max told his story. He finished his drink and led Max back to the table with the widows. "It was good to see you again. I'll be in touch soon."

"You do that. Now ladies, where were we?"

Bruce walked off when he heard the ladies giggle at Max's attention. He called Steve to let him know that the corporate office was moved to Edna's house, but other than that, Max had no pertinent information. He was going to be useless to them.

Steve went to see Janda the following morning and began by complimenting and trying to sweet-talk the pretty young secretary. Janda remained professional and listened to Steve but did not acknowledge his compliments.

"Sir, why did you stop by? What is your business with Chessmore Industries?"

Steve realized she wasn't going to be an easy target to distract. "Yes, well, I do have a serious request. We are missing a file at our office and wanted to find out if you may have seen it."

"It's hard to say since I have no idea who you are, why you're here, or what I would be looking for."

"I apologize. I'll start over. When I walked in, I was surprised by your beauty."

He gave her his most flirtatious smile, but he got no response as Janda sat staring at him. Steve pulled out a business card and handed it to her. The card read, *Hansen, Perry, Lincoln & Chessmore*.

"George was our partner, and we've been trying to locate one particular file. We didn't want to bother Edna while she was grieving, but since she has gone back to work, we thought we would ask her if George had some files here at the house. We'd be happy to go through his old files to locate it."

"I see. I don't have the authority to allow you access to anything. We will have to wait for Mrs. Chessmore to return."

"When will that be?"

"I have no idea."
"So are you aware of any files from our office?"
"Mister?"
"Perry. Steve Perry at your service."
"Mr. Perry. Let me remind you I am Mrs. Chessmore's personal secretary. I assist in running her office, nothing more. If you are missing files from your office, that is out of my jurisdiction. I think you need to leave now. I have another scheduled appointment in a few minutes."
"All right, but in case you come across the file, give me a call, all right?"
"Yes, sir, but I doubt very much I will run across anything. I have access to this office, a bathroom, and the kitchen. Unless someone stores something in any of those rooms, there will be no files found."
Steve let himself out and grumbled all the way to the car. "*Maybe Max is right. The snippy little secretary needs to be fired.*"

Mike listened and taped the whole conversation. He sent it on to Tom to listen to, and Mike had no doubt that the men arrested had come for whatever files the men wanted. After Janda left for the day, Jordan arrived to help Mike search the house. They spent the next four hours looking everywhere for any loose files that didn't pertain to Chessmore Industries.

"It's got to be in the safe. I wonder if the police ever got any information from those guys they arrested? Call Tom and see if he knows. He was going to keep an eye on the case."

Jordan gave Tom a call and got a chewing out for calling so late at night. He even heard his wife complaining in the background. No wonder Mike wanted him to call. He asked Tom about any evidence found on the men that showed they had the combination to the safe and was informed he would call him back in the morning.

Jordan popped over first thing the following morning to see Mike and gave him the combination for the safe. One of the men began talking to an FBI agent and never shut up. The trouble was, he didn't know the name of the man behind the orders because his so-called friend picked him up for the job and promised him lots of money to help pull it off. Tom's agent would continue to assist the local police in trying to get more information from the other man, but for now at least, they had the combination.

Mike decided to wait until Janda left, so there wouldn't be any questions as to why they were getting into the safe. He also asked Tom to arrive and watch so they had witnesses as to what they found, and that no one took anything. Jordan decided to hang out and eat whatever he could find, nap on the couch in Mike's room, or watch TV while he waited for Janda to go home for the day.

A few minutes after she left, Tom arrived. They went straight to the safe and opened it up without difficulty. Jordan took a video of the procedure for documentation in case something else came up missing. Outside of a few personal mementos, some cash, and the passports, there was nothing of interest.

Mike put everything back and hung the picture back in front

of it. He pondered a moment and then took the picture back down and reopened the safe. He quickly manipulated the combination and then locked it once again.

Tom asked, "What the heck did you just do?"

"Someone knew the code to the safe. There is a bunch of money in there, so I changed the code. I'm not telling anyone but Mrs. Chessmore when she finally returns."

Tom nodded. "Good idea. Well, we struck out."

"I'm telling you, that blip on the screen. Someone came in here and got to the safe before those knot heads tried."

"You could be right. But who?"

"That is the million-dollar question of the day." He didn't know how right he was.

******

James watched the Chessmore house from across the street in a grove of trees. He and his coworker Dave put up a tree stand so no one would notice them. It was so much safer and easier than sitting in a car. Dave took the night shift, and James watched during the day. The stand was large enough for them both to be there long enough to give each other report at the end of each shift. His buddy kept watch while he went into the house and grabbed the file from the safe. When James returned the next morning, Dave told him about the men being arrested a couple of hours after he went inside. James was glad he went in when he did. A couple of hours later, he would have been caught in the middle of everything, and it would have been disastrous. The file was safe, and a new plan was being devised.

James watched as Max went storming in and out of the house and then again when Steve Perry showed up. He chuckled when he also went storming out of the house. That secretary must be pretty good to tick both of those men off. He couldn't wait to meet her.

The two men waited several days to activate their plan. They wanted to make sure everyone was plenty nervous first. Guilty men made mistakes, and the more nervous they became, the more mistakes they were making. Once Steve Perry showed up at the house and left empty-handed, he knew it was time to get started. The men were definitely starting to make plenty of mistakes.

James headed back to the cabin. He always made sure the moon was behind clouds or no moon at all. That night was crucial, and he wanted no mistakes. He pulled into the driveway and made his way to the cabin, lights off. He rolled to a stop, pulled his cap down low over his forehead, checked his fake beard, and grabbed a light jacket. Stepping out, he went to the cabin door and knocked.

Sarah came to the door. "James. Good evening. We weren't expecting you tonight. I'll get our list."
She made to turn and leave, but James stopped her. "Sarah, wait. Could you do me a favor?"
"Sure."
"Have Mrs. Chessmore bring the list out. I'd like to visit with her. Out here. Please."

Sarah nodded, puzzled about the sudden change in procedure, but didn't ask why. She went back in the cabin.

and he could hear her call out to Edna. There were murmurs, but he couldn't make out the conversation. He walked over to the chairs on the porch and sat down to wait. Edna finally came out the door.

"Please shut the door, Mrs. Chessmore." She did and let her eyes adjust to the darkness. Once she noticed him sitting in a chair, she joined him. "Here's the list."

He took it and put it in his pocket. Quietly, he asked her, "I need to know that you trust me and that I am truly keeping you safe."

"It took me a while, but I do feel safe here. Especially after you brought the girls to me. I don't have to look over my shoulder, and when I look outside, I see peace and tranquility, not someone watching my every move. It's been a few years since I've felt this healthy, both physically and mentally. I suppose I should thank you for stealing me away, for whatever reason."

James watched her carefully, the dim glow of light from the window occasionally slashing across her face as she slowly rocked in her chair. "I need to ask you some questions that may be uncomfortable, but I think we can clean up a lot of things if I can find the answers. I'd like to be able to take you home again."

"Home. I do miss it, but it's so lovely here. Sarah and Martha love it too. We're having a wonderful time." She paused and stopped rocking. "Ask. I'll try to answer."

"I need you to think back to a long time ago. Say, maybe a year or two. I need you to think back to when your husband began to become overly stressed and more worried about something. I need to know if he shared his concerns with you or kept them to himself."

"What's this all about?" Tears welled up at the mention of George.

"Please. I know it's hard, but in order to complete my mission to keep you safe forever, I need more information from you."

Edna wiped away the tears and took a deep breath. "I blocked out a lot of memories the first six months after he died. I didn't want to think about it." She took another deep breath and sighed. "Okay. Let's see. George. Sweet George. We had thirty-two years together. We weren't always a happy couple, especially at the end, but that's life. We had a good marriage overall. We sang together, we danced together, went to church together, had a baby together, had careers together, and then he died and left me alone. It took me six long months to forgive him for it, but I finally got past it and then jumped right into the middle of whatever this is."

She paused and looked at the night sky. The clouds would pass long enough to see a vast number of stars twinkling so bright and close that Edna felt she could reach out and touch them. She got up and walked to the railing to get a better view.

"It was close to two years ago the first time George came home madder than a wet hen at his partners. He refused to tell me why, but he was absolutely livid. It all started to go downhill from there— calls late at night, meetings on weekends, paperwork he would stash away from my eyes. He kept telling me not to worry, that he had it handled. About six months before he died, he began to drink heavily. Never in our whole life had I ever seen him imbibe too much. We began to quarrel, and he drank more. George refused to tell me what the problems were and flat out told me to mind my own business. I walked away from him and moved into my own bedroom suite. I'm not sure he ever noticed."

She took a deep breath to continue. "A couple of months before he died, he said we needed to update our will. I agreed it was way past time to do so. You see, our only child died a couple of years earlier, and we had no one to leave the estate to. He arranged to use an outside lawyer, which I thought was strange. George said it was none of his partners' business what we did with our own estate, and he did have a point. I had no problem with the arrangements he wanted to make, so we set up the appointment. We were civil to each other around then, and he and I managed to attend a few dinner parties with friends without him drinking too much. The new will was put together without incident, and once it was completed, George seemed to calm down a little. The will was set up like most couples I know. If he died first, it all went to me or vice versa. Looking back, it was almost like he had a premonition about dying. He even arranged to have our accountants make sure the bills were paid every month, and a percentage of his income was put away in stocks and bonds. It was a simple arrangement, and I was grateful he thought about doing it since I was so busy with my own businesses. A few weeks later, he had a massive heart attack in the middle of supper with friends."

Edna was surprised that she wasn't bawling like a baby by then, but there were only a few tears. The cabin was slowly healing her, and she was grateful to James for bringing her to the mountain. James, sitting in the shadows, had tears rolling down his face. He couldn't talk in fear of sounding like he was choking up, and then he would have to explain himself. He took some deep, cleansing breaths.

"What happened to his business dealings and the office?"

Edna turned around to face him. "His partners bought his share out, took his clients, and paid the estate. They were shocked to find out we had a different lawyer and copies of the original contract in hand. Plus, George made a codicil to his will that stated that any legal contract made after the original partnership was drawn up was to be considered null and void and fraudulent and that he would not have and did not have any intention on changing the original partnership. I didn't even consider the ramifications of that until now. I remember our lawyer stating it was a good thing we had come to him when we did. He had to threaten a lawsuit to finalize the partnership buyout. It makes complete sense what with everything that is going on. George knew something wasn't right with his partners. He considered them lifelong friends, so it was no wonder he was upset."

"Were you aware of your husband keeping any work files at home?"

"Hmmm. Let me think." Edna was quiet a long time. You could hear the crickets chirping in the yard, the bullfrogs calling from the stream, and the rustling in the bushes and leaves. "I hadn't given it any thought, but I do remember one drunken night George pointed to the safe and said, *"It's all in there. All of it."* Then he passed out on the divan. I ignored him and went to bed. Do you think all of this time I was holding the key to his agony and didn't know it?"

"Yes, but he chose not to share it with you, and he

was right not to do so. That's why you're at the cabin and not at the house being harassed, or worse, for information you didn't know about. Once you found it, you might have died too."

"Do you think someone killed him?"

"Not literally, but it drove him into a heart attack. He should have come to me sooner."

"He told you about it?"

"Let's just say, by the time he chose to alert someone, it was too late to save him, but I'm here now and I'm going to make sure it doesn't happen again."

James got up and walked over to Edna, held her close, and hugged her tight. She clung to him for a long time.

"No one is going to hurt you or those women in there, you hear me?" he whispered. She nodded into his shoulder. He released her and headed for the car. "I'll be back in a few days." Then he was gone.

Edna stood on the porch and wept. A memory triggered as James held her, but she couldn't put her finger on it. Martha and Sarah came out to join her when Edna didn't come back in right away. The three of them stood holding each other by the waist for several minutes before they went back into the cabin one by one. Edna took one more look down the lane before closing the door.

When James hit the highway and could get cell phone coverage, he called Dave. "The plan is a go. Start getting everything lined up." As he drove back to the city, he thought of everything Edna said. It was a very emotional time, and he shouldn't have held her like that but he couldn't help it. He needed it as much as she did.

******

Bradley went to the local jail and asked to see Doris. He waited patiently while the matron went to get her. She was finally brought in, and he sat down across from her and introduced himself. Doris didn't recognize him from the board meetings.

"I'm Bradley Jenkins, or, as you might know me, JINX." Doris gasped, and Bradley rushed on. "I need to apologize for getting you involved in my scheme. I didn't do anyone any justice, including myself, and I messed up both your life and mine. I came to see you in person to apologize and ask for your forgiveness. I'm trying to make it all right again."

Doris had been sulking for days, believing she was the only one who would be in trouble for the money scheme. "Did you get caught?"

"Yes, and I'm going to the do the right thing. I'm selling out my corporation and getting everyone I owe paid back, including Mrs. Chessmore. I'll probably be broke by the time I'm done, but it won't matter. What matters is that I get you out of here. I'm so sorry you're still sitting in jail."

"It was my choice. I broke into the office trying to find the papers to cover up my tracks, and I got myself caught in the process. I'm serving my time for some minor offenses right now. The embezzlement charge hasn't even been brought up yet. I'm in no hurry because someone is threatening me, and the agents told me it wasn't you. Do you know who it is?"

Bradley shook his head. "I have no idea. I was asked the same question, but I'd never do that. All I did was help finagle the financial sheets to get the money and paid your bills. Do you have any idea who else it might be?"

"I don't know. I was just a secretary. Sure, I overstepped my bounds and ended up in trouble for it, but I got too big for my britches. I probably upset someone besides Mrs. Chessmore and didn't realize it."

"I'm sorry, Doris. You call me if you need something. I owe you."

He left his card with her, and Doris watched him leave. Her current sentence was coming to an end, and she had no idea if she would be safe at home or not. She hoped an agent would stop by and tell her so she could make plans one way or the other.

Bradley had an appointment at his lawyers to meet about selling his property and businesses. Mr. Marchman's lawyers sent over the agreement, and he reviewed it that day. They were going to expedite the deal, and Mr. Popoff hoped to complete all the transactions in four to six weeks if the agreement was satisfactory. Bradley dutifully notified his bookie of the sell off and promised the full amount of money due as soon as possible after the sale. He knew the bookie's men were keeping an eye on him, but then he also had an FBI agent keeping an eye on both of them.

Mr. Popoff and the agents worked out a deal where Bradley would continue to make things right and the agents would bring in the bad guys. In the end, Bradley was hoping for probation and no jail time, plus he wanted to get Doris out of jail without any further damage to her own reputation. The agents were hoping to get everyone involved in the extortion ring and shut it down.

He thought about his visit with Doris. When she walked in, he realized she had no memory of meeting him at the board meetings. He knew during those meetings she wasn't paying much attention to anything, and occasionally she took some notes. But she spent most of her time on her phone instead. In reality, she was a nice girl, but she was tempted by easy money, just as he had been. The difference was, she got nervous about it, and he just wanted more.

His gambling had become an obsession, and thousands of dollars later, he was personally broke. He'd even sold his house to pay off gambling debts and was now living in a small apartment. The only thing he'd been smart about was not touching the working capital of his corporation. He increased his personal wage, though, but it was never enough. Once he'd run through all his cash, cars, and homes, that was when he began the embezzlement scheme. Since he was on the board, he already had access to the financials, and it was easy to convince Doris to come along for the ride.

He was now going to lose everything he and his wife had worked so hard to establish. When he thought back, the trouble started after his wife died and the kids moved away. Loneliness set in, and he tried to find a substitute to get him out of the house for things besides work. It was time to pay the piper. Bradley wanted to make sure each of his kids got something once the sale went through, and then he would live frugally on whatever was left. Once he took care of his gambling debts and Mrs. Chessmore, that is. He was going to have to admit to his kids what he had done, but until everything was settled, Bradley didn't want to worry them needlessly.

He spent an hour at Mr. Popoff's office hammering out details of the sale and finally approved the agreement. A call was made, the contract faxed to Mr. Marchman's, and they waited for a return fax with his signature. They didn't have to wait long for it to return, and in four weeks the transfer of the corporation would be completed. Bradley picked up the letter the lawyer drafted for him, read it over, and nodded. He now had a duty to notify all the offices of the pending sale and let his own business office know they were closing down. The letter would go out to them immediately. It was a bittersweet moment for him but necessary.

******

Maxamillian spent several days worrying about Edna's disappearance and knew he wouldn't be going back to her house and approach her snippy secretary again. He finally decided to go to one of her other offices and spied a couple of people that used to be at Edna's corporate office. He asked if it would be all right to visit with them, and since many of the Edna's secretaries had met him previously, they agreed it would be fine.

He made his way over to one of the men and asked if he knew where Edna was. He said he hadn't heard a thing about her but was happy he had been moved to this location. It was twenty minutes closer from home, and had some real pretty girls working there. Max tolerated the man's chatter for a while then interrupted him.

"Have you seen anything out of Doris?"

"No, man. She was fired and then got arrested for B&E at the office. She's cooling her heels at the county jail."

"What?"

"Yeah. She went nuts when Mrs. Chessmore was gone the first time and thought she was the boss. When Mrs. Chessmore returned, she refused to give up the reins. Crazy lady, anyway."

Max thanked the guy for the information, turned and headed for his car, got in, and drove straight to the county jail. He asked to see Doris and was told he'd have to wait approximately one hour before she could be brought up for a visit. He was an impatient man but said he would wait.

Doris was finally brought to the visitor's room one and a half hours later, and Max was just about ready to go nuts. He'd read every magazine in the waiting room by then. He was taken to the visitor room, and Doris was sitting there quietly checking out her nails. It looked to Max like she'd chewed them all to the nubs.

She looked up at him when he came to the table. "What do you want?"

Max sat down and gave her his signature smile. "I got word you were here and came to see if I could help."

"Help what?"

"You, of course. Do you need bail money or

anything?"

Doris sighed. "Man. I'm tired of telling people that I'm serving my time. It's almost done. Why can't everyone just leave me alone?"

"Has Edna been to see you?"

"See me? Why would she come here? I broke into the office and trashed the place."

"So you didn't know she went somewhere for a while?"

"I don't know why you'd think I'd know anything. I've been in here for weeks."

"Just checking. Are you sure I can't do something for you? Get your job back with Edna maybe?"

"You're crazy, man." Doris jumped up and asked the guard to let her leave. Max sat there and stared at her back as she left the room. He'd gotten nowhere today.

******

Mrs. Whethers continued to come to see Janda weekly. Business was booming, and at the last board meeting everyone agreed the financials were stable after Carson Shoemaker gave his report. Bradley resigned from the board early that evening and excused himself from the rest of the meeting. He cited personal responsibilities that required his immediate attention and thanked everyone for allowing him to serve with them. The board went into a special session and devised a short list of people for Janda to call and ask if they had an interest in serving as Bradley's replacement.

When Mrs. Whethers arrived for her next visit, Janda reported to her that there were several people interested and would be available. They would have special meetings set up to interview each person, and Mrs. Whethers would choose one of them to come to the next board meeting and be elected as the replacement for Bradley. After Mrs. Whethers signed the last of the checks, she sat back and looked at Janda.

"I must say, you are a remarkable young woman keeping everything running. I'm very proud of you. Edna would be proud of you too. Speaking of Edna, have you heard from her?"

"Not a peep. Thank you for the compliment. I fell into this job accidentally after she fired Doris, and all she asked was that I do the job and be loyal to her. I've had to learn the job flying by the seat of my pants, but I really enjoy the challenges. I'm happy that you believe I'm doing a good job, though. I wasn't sure I'd like it at first, but this has been an amazing experience. I'm glad Mike is still here to help out occasionally."

"Mike? Oh yes. That man at the first meeting. I didn't realize he was still involved."

"Oh yes. He's had to help me by removing obnoxious people out of my office. I'm glad to have him around. This is a mighty big house, and I don't worry about being here by myself working knowing he is always close by somewhere."

"I hadn't thought about you being here alone. Very good then. I'll leave you to your work, which is truly excellent."

"Thank you, Mrs. Whethers. I'll see you next week."

Janda sat back and smiled. She was working hard, and it was finally paying off. She loved her job and continued to learn more about Chessmore Industries every day. Carson Shoemaker answered her questions quickly, and the managers of all the businesses were very helpful and considerate. Working for Mrs. Chessmore was definitely a blessing.

Mike hung out at the house during Janda's work hours, and ran his errands once she left for the day. He was trying to pick up some odd jobs to keep him busy during the day, but he heard Janda visiting with Mrs. Whethers about how grateful she was to have him around. Instead, he found two additional businesses that required cameras to be installed and their business monitored at night. No one wanted him around during the day while the employees were there anyway, so the jobs fit right into his schedule. He could monitor them at night from the comfort of his suite at Mrs. Chessmore's, and nap during the day while Janda worked. It was a win-win for them both because he was actually getting a paycheck. He still didn't feel right billing Mrs. Chessmore for his hours. He decided his payment was living in the house protecting Janda and monitoring the system.

Jordan stopped by occasionally to check on things, but Mike knew he liked raiding the refrigerator more than seeing him. He was busy with his own jobs and occasionally took a quick nap on Mike's couch before heading out. Janda had lunch with Mike once in a while, and she thanked him for helping with her disgruntled visitors.

"I just wanted you to know it was appreciated."
"No problem, Janda. Just holler if you need anything."

He always left his door open, and Janda always left the office door open. She let him know if someone was at the gate that she either wasn't expecting or she didn't know. He would monitor the conversation from his room and would only intervene if she became upset.

******

Gregory met with the trio of lawyers at his office a couple more times in the following weeks. The men were more nervous about no one seeing Edna than their other problems. People were beginning to talk, and soon the whole town would be gossiping about her disappearance. No one knew where she went, and talk among the servants was that her cook and maid were missing too.

"Men, we need to get a handle on all of this. Our careers are on the line. We had nothing to do with her disappearance, so why are you worried about it?" said Gregory.

Bruce broke into the conversation. "Look. We can all lose our license to practice. That's everything to us. If Edna found that file, she's probably got this whole thing figured out by now and turned us all in."

The other two men agreed. Mark Lincoln had always been the quieter of the partners. He sat and watched but rarely interrupted. Today was different. "George was right, you know. We're all screwed."

Gregory looked over at all of them. "I'm headed over to her house right now. I'm done with all of you because you can't get anything done. We need Edna, and we need her now." He jumped up and headed out the door. The others watched him go, but no one wanted to follow.

Mark said softly, "I tell you, we're all screwed."

The men got up, and Karen watched them go. Mark told her thank you on his way out.

Gregory was let in through the gates after announcing himself, and he ambled into the house like he owned it. Janda waited for him in the hallway and led him to the office.

As they both settled in, she asked, "What can I do for you?"

"I'm an associate of Mrs. Chessmore's, and I haven't seen her for months. I demand to know where she is."

"I see. You and a million others, including me."

Gregory gave Janda his hardened stare in hopes to make her very nervous, but Janda stared back. She reminded him of a younger version of his own secretary, Karen. "So you're telling me that a little ole' secretary is running the show all this time?"

Janda hated condescension, but knew it was typical of people who liked to throw their weight around. "Chessmore Industries is currently run by a CEO. Maybe you'd like to discuss your business with her? I can make you an appointment next week if you'd like?"

Gregory jumped up and paced the room. "This makes absolutely no sense whatsoever. No one has any idea where she is, and no one from Chessmore Industries seems to care about it. Why don't we read it in the papers about her missing? Is she dead or something?"

Janda cringed at that statement, got up, and walked to the office door. "Mr. Marchman, thank you for your concern, but I believe it's time for you to go."

"Don't tell me what to do. You're awfully impertinent for a secretary. Steve said you should be fired, and I can see why."

"Excuse me?"

"You heard me. I'll leave when I'm good and ready to go. I expect to get some answers right now, and I expect you to give them to me."

About that time Janda heard a welcome voice behind her. "I believe you are ready to leave, Mr. Marchman, and I'd be happy to escort you to the door."

"Listen, buster. I don't know who you are, but I came here to get answers and I expect to get them."

Mike calmly walked into view, shoulder holster in place and a hand on the butt of his gun. "If I'm not mistaken, you are ready to go now, or I will have to take matters into my own hands."

Gregory was livid that he was being threatened. "Do you know who I am?"

"Of course, but as you can plainly see, we don't care and you've been asked nicely to leave several times. The next step is up to you." He nodded at Janda who went directly to the phone and dialed 911.

"I'm calling from the Chessmore residence. We have Mr. Marchman here, and he has refused to leave the premises and is causing quite a ruckus." She paused. "Thank you."

Looking at the men who were staring at each other, she said, "They're on their way."

Gregory turned to Janda. "You haven't heard the last of me." He stormed out of the house, and Janda dropped into her chair to wait for the police. "Thanks, Mike."

She faced him with a questioning look on her face. "So. Where is Mrs. Chessmore?"

Mike looked back at her. "I don't know, but I think it's time to tell you what I do know." He spent the next hour going over everything that had happened in the last couple of months. "Now you know as much as I do, but you can't tell anyone she is missing. She told Mr. Harrison that she was going away on personal business, and we just have to hope that's what she is doing. I have no idea where Martha and Sarah are either. In the meantime, we have to take care of business, so when she returns there is something to return to."

Gregory jumped into his car and sped down the Chessmore driveway and out onto the street. He almost hit another car while flying around the corner to leave the estate, but he never slowed down. He barreled on toward his own home and tore up his access road like the devil was chasing him. In reality, it probably was.

He made a few calls while pacing the floor. An alarm went off to notify him someone entered his access road, and he went to the window to see who it was. *"Great .Now what?"* He hung up the phone in the middle of the conversation and watched the police cruiser arrive. Gregory opened the front door and waited while two officers got out of the car and came up the steps.

"Good afternoon, Officers. May I help you?"
"Mr. Marchman, we've received a complaint from Chessmore Industries. I'm sure you're aware of the incident."
"Yes, but I'm sure it was just a misunderstanding."
"We're here to inform you that you are no longer welcome at their headquarters, and if it continues, you will

be seeing us again under less than friendly circumstances."

"I assure you I won't be returning."

"Very well. Thank you for your time. Now, if you will excuse us?" The men turned to get in their cruiser.

Gregory shut the door and walked back to the window to watch them leave the premises. Once he got this mess cleaned up, he'd find out who that man was at the Chessmore house and make sure he understood that no one treats Gregory Marchman like a thug.

******

Mike copied the recording from the Marchman visit and sent it off to Tom. Things were coming together, and now they could put Marchman and the attorneys together. He felt the net was closing and wished he could be in on whatever would be going down. Things were turning ugly, and he hoped Janda didn't get hurt in the meantime. He hoped Mrs. Chessmore would show up safe and sound at the end of the day, too.

******

James received word it was almost time to move in. Thankfully, it would come to a close for everyone concerned. He was tired of chasing prey and never catching it. Always a step behind, he could almost grasp success. Watching Gregory Marchman storm out of the house, he knew things were falling apart for the man.

He continued to make his weekly runs to the cabin and reassured the women that the mission was getting close to being completed and to have a little more patience. Edna would just remark, *"Be safe, young man."* Only one other person knew where the women were tucked away, and if he couldn't return to get them home, his supervisor would.

******

Bradley, his lawyer, and the Marchman team met and finalized all the paperwork. He immediately went to the bank to make sure the money was actually there. Bradley visited with the bank manager to transfer funds to a special account for his kids. He put it in their name only to make sure that if his gambling ways struck again, there would be no way to touch it.

Then he had a cashier's check made out for the amount owed to the bookies. Bradley, embarrassed by the withdrawal, confessed to the banker what mistakes he made by betting on the horses. He could write his own personal check to Chessmore Industries for the amount he took from Edna. That would, at face value, look legitimate for the accountant.

He went home to write the check and enclosed a note for the secretary to give it straight to the accountants, as they would know where the money belonged. Bradley didn't want to involve any more people into the embezzlement issue, but knew during his arrest that the CPA was well aware of the disappearance. Once he had the check ready to mail, he called the agent assigned to him and told him he was ready to pay his bookie. They arranged the site, Bradley called and set the time, and then notified the agent when he'd be there.

Bradley sat nervously waiting for someone to show up. There were a couple of men having coffee and more outside in the parking lot. His legs were shaking, and he kept tapping the table and glancing out the window. Finally, someone sat down beside him and quietly said, "I'm here for the money."

Bradley nodded and slowly pulled the cashier's check out of his shirt pocket. The men having coffee got up to leave. He handed over the check; the man looked at it, nodded, and left the shop. Bradley watched him leave along with several other cars in the parking lot. He was so nervous it took a few minutes for him to calm down enough to get up and go home. He took a deep breath and hoped he could put this all behind him now.

The agents followed discreetly behind the deliveryman. Once they knew the location, they called the site in. The agents backed off and waited for the man to leave the house. They arranged for the local police department to pick him up once he had driven a few blocks from the drop-off site. The FBI wanted things to look like a normal stop so they didn't alert anyone to what they were really up to by arresting him right at the end of the driveway. They successfully pulled off that part of the mission, and once the man was in FBI custody and locked up, he was interrogated by federal agents.

The man denied knowing anything, but he also didn't request a lawyer. Basically, he refused to cooperate at all. The agents decided to hold him and let him think about things for a while before readdressing the issue with him. With the mission coming up, they decided to detain him until everyone else was arrested and find out if he would talk then. When your money man was in jail, they felt there would be several people talking.

The following day, James walked into the FBI office, introduced himself, and asked to see Agent Tom Edwards. He was brought to his office, and he introduced himself to Tom. "We need to talk."

Several conference calls and two hours later, Tom requested that all agents assigned to Mrs. Chessmore's recovery, plus the extortion task force, meet in the report room in an hour. By then, Dave joined James and brought along another four men with him. By the time the group got together, there were more than thirty men in the room waiting to see what had brought them all together. Dave and James, along with their men, stood off to the side and watched as everyone came in and found a seat. Tom remained standing at the front of the room, casually leaning on the podium. Once everyone was settled, Tom began talking.

"Let's get the ball rolling here. As you know, we are close to arresting and shutting down an extortion and betting ring. This morning, I had a visit from the AG's office. As you may already know, they oversee our department and have had their own group of men involved in this case, unbeknownst to us until now." There were a few grumbles in the room due to not being let in on information beforehand. Tom held up his hand for quiet.

"I understand the concern, but let me get on with this. The AG's office has been tracking the extortionists for several years and has been unable to crack this case until their office got a tip several months ago from a private citizen. Before they could pursue it, that person died. In the meantime, several things popped up on our side, and we are now involved in the same case. After several conversations with the AG and the men standing along the wall there, we are joining forces and will make one massive swing through and arrest as many people on our list as possible."

At the mention of the other men in the room, several of the agents glanced over at them. The men along the wall nodded at the agents. "I'm going to let one of them come up and discuss the details as they know it today. Gentlemen?"

Dave came forward, and Tom moved farther away, but remained in the room for possible questions. "I'm Dave Huber. As Tom said, we've been tracking the extortionists for years, but haven't been able to get enough names to make a case. We knew it involved some high-priority names, but the runners we would arrest never talked. Many of the men hired for going after people that couldn't pay up were thugs with records a mile long. The trend, you may have noticed, is that once someone is arrested and they don't talk, they get paid a bonus, and then they disappear from the scene. On occasion, we find they pop up in another city doing the same thing. A couple of years ago, a private citizen began to track something he noticed and had a gut feeling it wasn't a good thing. He kept names, dates, financial records, the works, and locked it up. Once he felt he had enough information, he notified the AG's office and was going to meet me at an arranged time to turn the paperwork over. It didn't happen because he died suddenly."

Dave paused and looked around and glanced over at James. James nodded, and Dave continued.

"Our plan was to wait until the widow mourned for a

few months, and when we felt it was time, we would make an appointment to see her and ask for the information. As you may have gathered by now, that person is Mrs. Chessmore. The extortion ring and Mrs. Chessmore's case are directly related to each other because all of those people are trying to get the same information we have. So now we need to work together to lay out a plan to make sweeping arrests across the country, all at the same time, so as to not alert anyone else. You will be directly involved locally, and our office will arrange groups of agents in other cities. Are there any questions?"

"Yes. How did you get the information if Mrs. Chessmore is missing?"

"Let's just say that we have our ways." The agents talked among themselves, and finally Tom got their attention. "We're going to put up a list of names and places and decide when and how we are going in for the arrest. The AG's office will work with the other cities. The top dogs are elsewhere, and we need to make sure they get caught. Let's get to work."

Tom wrote the list of names on the board that they were going to search for and arrest. Dave and James, along with their men, left and headed for Washington DC to make plans of their own. James went to the cabin the night before to check on the women and brought them extra grocery items. He had no idea when or if he would return for the women and take them home.

******

Doris served her time, and there still were no charges against her for embezzlement. As she was signing for her personal items, she looked around, wondering if there was anyone watching for her at the apartment and if she would still be threatened once home. Doris took her belongings and was glad to finally hear she was free to go, but warily walked out the door and down the street. The police told her that her car was locked up and she had to pay a fine to get it out, but without a job, she knew there was no way she'd have the money to get it released. Not after all that time.

She passed by a library, stopped, and walked back through the door. The librarian glanced at her but went back to work at the desk. Doris sighed, walked to the lady, and asked if she could use the phone to catch a ride since she had no car available.

The lady looked at her and nodded to the one across the desk. Doris found the card that Bradley Jenkins gave her and dialed his number. It rang several times before he picked up.

"Hello?"
"This is Doris. I need a ride. I'm at the city library."
"Doris. You're out. I'll be happy to come and get you. Stay right there."

Doris thanked the librarian and decided to wait outside in the fresh air. It had been a long time, and she didn't care that the sun was beating down. There was a bench under a tree that she could sit and watch the traffic go by and wait for Bradley to show up. She knew it would be a while but didn't care. *"I'm free"*, she thought.

It was a good half an hour before Bradley picked her up, but she was happy to have a ride. "How are you? I'm so glad you're out. Where is your car?"

"It's in the impound yard, and I have to pay a bunch of money to get it out."

"Oh no. Let's get over there before they close."

"It won't do any good. I don't have the money it takes to get it released anyway."

"I'll pay for it. Don't you worry about it."

"I'm sure it will be a lot of money. I've been locked up a long time."

"It's all right. I got everyone paid back and have a little money stashed away now. It's the least I can do."

Doris finally agreed because she could see no other option at the time. Bradley helped Doris fill out all the paperwork that was required and wrote the check to get the car released. A few minutes later, a man drove her car up to the door and handed her the keys.

"Thank you," Doris said to the man. She turned to Bradley. "Thank you for picking me up and helping me with all of this."

"No problem, Doris. What are you going to do now?"

"I have no idea. I also don't know if I'm going to be threatened. That worries me. Do you have any idea if the cops are ever going to charge me with embezzlement?"

"I don't think you have to worry about the embezzlement charge, but I'm not one hundred percent sure. I don't even know for sure what they are going to get me for. I paid all the money back and helped the FBI catch someone, so I'm hoping for probation. I haven't heard either way. As far as being threatened, if you are, make sure you contact the police right away. They'll want to know."

"All right. Well, thanks again."

"Doris, you have my card. Call me if you need me, okay?" Bradley smiled at her.

"Thanks. I will." Doris smiled back and felt like there was one person she could depend on, even if it was the one that helped get her into trouble to begin with.

Doris got in the car and made sure she had enough gas to get home. Thankfully, she had put some gas in it a few days before her arrest. She turned the car for home and wondered what she was going to do for a job now that she had a record. No one would trust her to run an office since Mrs. Chessmore fired her. She decided she better hit the streets the next day because she knew her checking account held very little reserve.

She went up to her apartment and checked her surroundings. Everything looked the same, so she unlocked the door and stood in the doorway looking at the messy apartment. The apartment smelled like rotten garbage. She immediately opened up some windows and wrapped up the kitchen garbage, emptied the refrigerator, and took everything to the dumpster. Finding some deodorizer, she filled the apartment with spray. Doris waited outside for a little bit until the spray smell diminished. As she waited, she watched the kids on the playground and the cars coming and going in the parking lot. Everything seemed the same, but she felt different. Entering the apartment, she decided to spend the rest of the afternoon cleaning up the place before taking a shower. Double bolting the door, she got busy.

The apartment was spic and span and smelled much better. Doris hadn't realized what a slob she had become. Before heading for the shower, she grabbed her cell phone and plugged it in to charge. Her mother was probably livid that she hadn't been called. That wasn't going to be a pleasant visit, no matter what the reason, but Doris decided she was going to have to fess up to her stupidity. She headed for the shower and hoped that her mother would eventually forgive her.

She got online and checked her account balance and figured she could go buy a few groceries. Thankfully, Mrs. Chessmore had paid her the extra money as promised. Before leaving the apartment, she checked her phone. It was half charged, and she saw several phone messages, hundreds of texts, and who knew how many other messages had been left. She put the phone down and decided to handle it after supper.

It felt good to fix a meal at home. Doris had a light supper and sat drinking a cold glass of iced tea on her balcony, enjoying the sounds of the evening. Her phone was charged, and now the decision needed to be made who to contact first. She briefly went through several messages and decided her crazy friends probably didn't care whether she got back to them or not. Hands down, she knew she had to call her mother. *"Here goes nothing."* Doris dialed home, and when her mother answered, she said, "Hi, Mom. I need to tell you something."

******

Bradley spent the previous weeks closing up the office and selling off desks and cabinets. He went to visit his kids and told them what he had done. Once the hard conversation was over, he reassured them that he wouldn't gamble again. He wasn't quite old enough to retire, but felt that there was enough money saved now that he could if he chose to. The last thing he wanted to do was to get bored and find himself back at the tracks. Looking at the want-ads one morning over breakfast, he saw an ad for a private optometrist's office. Bradley called them immediately to set up an interview time. It was back to where he started, but it would be enough. He hoped he could nail the job and get back into a routine. The office told him to stop by that afternoon, and he was happy to do so. When the owner realized who Bradley was, he had no problem offering him a job.

"I'm glad you sold out and decided to go back to work. I hope you don't get too bored here. I seem to be picking up some of your old business because some of the customers aren't as happy with the new owners."

"That's too bad. Not for you, of course, but I spent most of my life building that business. I hope I can help you build yours. It's funny. I don't miss the stress of the corporation. I think working for you will be just right."

"I hope so. How about we get some paperwork done and you can come to work as soon as you're ready."

"Let's do it."

Bradley filled out the paperwork and visited with his new boss before leaving. They hit it off immediately and decided it was meant to be working for someone else.

"One more thing. Do you know anyone that we could hire to help answer the phones and make appointments? I need one more girl in the front office."

Bradley smiled. "I know just the person. I'll start work on Monday and tell her to meet us here."

"Wonderful."

They shook hands, and Bradley walked out of the office to the car, whistling a tune. He dialed Doris and asked her if she had found a job. Since her answer was no, he excitedly said, "Well, you do now." Then he explained how they would both have a job on Monday. She fretted over what they would say when she filled out her paperwork.

"Doris, it's not a felony, just a misdemeanor, and you are allowed to make mistakes in life. I'll handle it. You used to be Mrs. Chessmore's right-hand person, so you will be able to handle this job. You won't get paid as much, but it's a paycheck. Tell me you'll do it."

"If you say so, but if they give me a hard time, I'm outta' there."

"They will appreciate the help, and I'll be there. No one will pick on you. They are lovely people."

"Okay, tell me the address, and I'll meet you bright and early Monday morning." Both Doris and Bradley were smiling ear to ear from their good luck.

******

At the next board meeting, Carson Shoemaker was given the check from Bradley. Janda said, "I don't know what this is for, but the note said to give it to you directly and you would know what to do with it. I've been holding it for a couple of weeks to give it to you at this meeting."

"Thank you, Janda. I know exactly what to do with it. I'll visit with Mrs. Whethers after the meeting."

Janda nodded and everyone settled in to start the meeting. Shortly after the meeting, Carson, who had been waiting in the office after his portion of the meeting, took Mrs. Whethers to the side and asked her to stay for a little while to talk once everyone was gone. He then went back to the office and waited.

When Mrs. Whethers made sure everyone was gone except Janda, Carson asked Janda to wait in the other room while they talked. She shut the doors and went to work cleaning up after the meeting. Carson handed the check over to Mrs. Whethers to look at.

"Good grief. That's a lot of money. What the heck is Bradley giving that to Chessmore Industries for?"

"To make a long story short, he skimmed it off the books, but he paid it back."

"You're kidding me. Is he in jail for this?"

"To my knowledge, no, but he sold his business and paid all his debts, including this one. I'm not sure what his sentence will end up being."

"You knew about this all along?"

"Yes, but Edna told me to be quiet because of everything going on, and she was trying to find the person who took the money. I originally put the stolen amount on the books as owner withdrawal until we could figure out what else to do with it. Now that he paid it back, I can go back in and adjust the books accordingly. I just needed you to know that the financials are going to change. Because Edna asked me to be quiet about it, I can't go back on my word at this point and tell anyone. Next month, I will just explain to the board that an audit was completed and the figures were corrected. I don't know what else we can do until Edna returns and tells me otherwise. Do you agree with it?"

"I hope none of this is illegal—I mean, changing the books."

"I can put an addendum on the records that shows what really happened. If we are ever audited by anyone else, the explanation will be there. I just don't think Edna wanted everyone on the board to know she was taken advantage of while she was gone after her husband died."

"As long as you make sure it's all legal, I'm all right with it. I'll leave it up to you to explain the financials to the board."

"By the way, you are doing a great job with the company."

"Thank you, but that little Janda is a spitfire, and I really think you should thank her instead."

"I will. Thank you for your time. I guess we better go and let Janda get everything locked up."

The three of them walked to their cars and headed for home. Mike was sitting in his office listening in to the conversation. He couldn't help himself. It's what he did for a living, and life had been good to him because of that for several years. He sat back, and his mind wandered as he scanned the computer screens from one business to another, not paying much attention to the picture in front of him. There would be an alarm if someone entered after hours, but he wasn't paid to rely on alarms. After all, someone slipped by the alarm once at the Chessmore estate, and he was still kicking himself for that one.

He thought about how he hadn't kept Mrs. Chessmore safe, and then the servants disappeared. Once again, he felt like he fell down on the job when he knew someone else had broken into the house and disarmed the video feed long enough to presumably unlock the safe. He was feeling pretty disgruntled with his carelessness and seriously considered hanging up his hat and retiring.

Mike's savings wasn't that great, but he could manage. He really enjoyed wandering the rose garden and working out in Mrs. Chessmore's exercise room, but it would end soon. If he gave up staying at the house, he would need to find someone to stay with Janda during the day or have the office moved elsewhere. It wasn't his decision to make really, but he stayed much longer than necessary. He was only there because Janda needed him on occasion. At least he had been of some service for someone at the Chessmore estate.

Jordan had been very busy with his own work in recent weeks, and Mike hadn't seen much of him. There wasn't anything new to discuss anyway. He began to scan through some of his video footage and began considering his options. Retirement was looking better all the time.

******

Karen set up another meeting with the three lawyers and Gregory Marchman. This had been a weekly meeting lately, and there was never a happy ending. Everyone always left angry, and Mr. Marchman always stormed out to meet with someone else. That someone else was the mayor, and they met behind closed doors at his office frequently. Karen kept meticulous records over the years, and as the men were yelling behind closed doors once again, she made a backup of her computer once again. There was something wrong, and she wanted no part of it.

Hansen, Perry, and Lincoln left for the afternoon, and Gregory Marchman stayed behind. Karen found him staring out his windows with his hands behind his back.

"Excuse me. Do you want me to cancel your next meeting?"
Gregory turned around, his face in a deep frown. "Who is it?"
Karen looked at her appointment book. "A Mr. Huber. He wanted to discuss a possible buyout on some property by the waterfront."
"I'll see him."

He turned back to the windows and began to look for all of his properties. He began to relax as he counted and then smiled when he had to find the new acquisitions from the optometry corporation he recently bought. Gregory was deep in thought when Karen buzzed that his appointment was ready. He still hadn't located the last two offices but shrugged his shoulders. "*There's always tomorrow.*"

"Have him come in."

Dave Huber walked in, wearing a crisp gray suit with a bright red tie. His shoes were shined so bright the sun glistened off them. He reached out his hand as he walked across the room to meet Gregory.

"I say, what a magnificent view you have from up here." They shook hands, and Dave moved right into his spiel. "I'm Dave Huber, and I've wanted to meet you for a long time. My company has been purchasing property by the waterfront for several years and I wondered if you were interested in building condos or guest homes in the area. Kind of a rebuilding and remaking of the waterfront is what I had in mind. Right now, there is a bunch of rundown warehouses that need burned or tore down and they are really an eyesore. I'd sell the land at a premium, and you could eventually make a killing. I'm not into the rebuilding part myself."

"That's an interesting proposition. Have a seat." After discussing how much land Dave's company owned, Gregory asked, "So why do you want to sell it now?"

"I've been hanging on to it for some time. I believe there is the perfect amount of land to make a whole new neighborhood, and I don't think the value will ever be more than I'm asking without improvements. I've been refused the change in zoning several times. The time is right for selling, and I can get my money back and go and invest in more property elsewhere. The only thing would be getting the city to agree with the change from industrial to residential or whatever you wanted to use it for."

"I can get any permit I want around here. I didn't get to where I am by having to wait in line for permits. I'd like to take a swing by and look at things before I agree to it."

"No problem. You sure you can get the city to change the zoning?"

"All it takes is a phone call, and it's done. The mayor

and I understand each other."

"Wonderful. I have to go for now. I'll call you in a week or so and set up a tour of the place."

"You can just leave me the address."

"Nope. The way my company works is, we show the property ourselves. The buyer takes it or leaves it at the time. I'm lining up buyers and you're first on the list, but I'll have several others by the time I call you back."

"Leave the name of your company with my secretary, please. I'll look forward to your call."

Dave saluted and left the room, shutting the door behind him. "Karen, I believe?"

"Yes, sir?"

"You have a lovely day."

"Thank you," she said as he walked out the door.

A few minutes later, Gregory came out of the office and asked Karen what the name of the company was.

"What company?"

"I asked that Huber fellow to leave you the name of his company."

"All he said was for me to have a lovely day."

Gregory began cussing and went back to his office, slamming the door behind him. *"Conceited fool. He can forget seeing me again."*

Dave made a few phone calls on the way to the airport. It was his last job before going back to Washington DC. He smiled as he headed through the terminal toward his gate. Yes, things were looking pretty good right now.

PART FOUR

Agents from all over the country were waiting in anticipation to make a sweep of corrupt men and women in all sectors of society. Each local police department would assist in the arrests and hold each individual until they could be processed and taken through the federal court system. Agent Tom Edwards and his men were to play an extensive role in the process, and he met with his men regularly to make sure they had all of their bases covered.

Dave called Tom every day, and they discussed the process and mulled over changes. Finally, the day arrived. Hopefully by five o'clock that evening, they would have multiple people arrested and no one would get hurt in the process. An hour before the start time, the agents spread out across the city and had themselves in place. Tom was notified everyone was ready and their targets were in sight. Tom made a quick call to Dave and told him they were ready. Dave nodded to James, and he left with his men for his own assignment. Dave called their supervisor and told him everyone was in place. Their supervisor would meet James at his location to assist in the arresting process, and Dave headed out with his group of agents.

At three p.m. eastern time, the arrests began. Tom entered the mayor's office, handed him a search warrant, and then proceeded to arrest both him and his secretary. They left with the mayor blubbering about police brutality. Another team walked into the lawyer's office, handed a search warrant to the secretary, and asked all three partners to come out of their offices.

Bruce Hansen was the most vocal and threatened lawsuits. Steve Perry attempted to talk his way out of the handcuffs, but Mark Lincoln came quietly and said he'd be happy to discuss whatever they wanted to know. In both offices, once their rights were read, computers and servers were confiscated, and locked files were hauled to a U-Haul truck sitting in front waiting for them.

Gregory Marchman was standing at his window locating each of his holdings when he heard someone arrive and talk to his secretary. The next thing he knew, there were three men in the office, cuffing him and reading him his rights. As he was led out of the office, he noticed his secretary loading a box with personal items. She ignored her boss as he was led out of the office and made sure the police had everything they would need before locking up behind them. Her efficiency made short work for everyone, including herself. All she asked was that she had time to write herself one last paycheck to get her by. Karen was so cooperative they couldn't deny her that request. She thought a moment and gave herself six months' severance pay, figuring she deserved that for putting up with Gregory's nonsense all these years.

Karen took the check, purse, a box of personal items and walked to the door. The men grabbed her backup disc, computer, and server and followed. She looked behind her at the stripped-down office and sighed, closed the door, and headed for the bank.

Dave walked into Senator Faustman's office and held out the search warrant. The secretary buzzed her boss, but by then Dave and his men started in the door. Down the hall, the same experience was happening in three other offices. This was not going to be good for the senator's careers, but Dave didn't care at this point. You could hear a lot of blustering and yelling going on, and it was drawing a crowd. There were always reporters close by, and they were flocking to the noise and taking lots of pictures.

The agents shoved by the mikes without talking and let the senators make all the noise they wanted. It was hard for Dave to keep a straight face and worked to add an extra-large frown to keep from smiling. He thought, "*What a circus.*" Leading everyone out of the office building, other agents took care of the search warrant and followed protocol every step of the way. There was no way they would be caught on camera not doing things properly.

James and two other agents headed into the offices of Hank Elliot. He had been making a name for himself in the racketeering business the last twenty years, but no one could ever pin anything on him. It was time for that to change, and James had a personal reason to make it happen. They walked in, and his supervisor and other agents were outside to help. Hank always had plenty of men around him, and all the agents knew this could be a bad situation. James led his men through the front door, and they dropped the search warrant on the secretary's desk.

"Please take yourself outside to one of our men. Hold your hands up as you go so they don't shoot you. Okay?" She nodded and took off for the open door, hands in the air. The men then walked to the office door, stood to the side, and threw the door open. "Gentleman, come on in."

The men quickly went through the door, guns drawn. The window behind Hank showed agents arresting other men and women while additional agents kept an eye on their surroundings.

As James came through the door, Hank took a double take. "It's you. I thought I killed you years ago."
"Well, you missed. Today we plan on taking you in."
"Funny guy. I won't make it easy, you know."

Before Hank finished talking, gunfire erupted, and everyone looked out the window. James saw his supervisor go down. He looked back to Hank just as the gun went off multiple times. The agents fired back, and Hank went down. James' last thought as he lay on the floor bleeding was of the women on the mountain. No one knew where they were except him and his supervisor, and they would never get down the mountain now. He tried to tell one of the other agents, but he couldn't get the words out. As he tried to formulate a sentence, he fell into a black void.

Across the states, similar incidents were happening in judge's chambers, mayor's offices, regular businesses, and people they used as runners and errand boys. On occasion they arrested a few other lawyers. In total, the sweep netted over fifty people, which in itself would make headline news. The only casualties that occurred happened at Hank Elliot's headquarters.

******

Edna, Martha, and Sarah found themselves in a ritual of walking the grounds more than once a day and enjoyed sitting on the porch. They played board games and cards outside when it was nice and occasionally started a fire to relax by on chillier evenings. The cabin was sitting high enough in elevation that the nights turned cool and the heat of the day was usually very pleasant. That evening, the women settled down after supper and watched the evening news. They were grateful for the satellite TV so they could keep up on the national news. Tonight, they were riveted to the TV as it played several scenes of the arrests over and over again.

Edna looked around. "Girls, I'm betting this was what James was talking about. Maybe we get to go home now." Martha and Sarah, always the conspiracy theorists, began to ramble off stories about what really happened and why. By the time they were through, all three of them were laughing so hard tears were flowing down their faces. "I think I'd hate to leave here," Edna said. "But I do miss home. How about you, girls?" They both agreed that they missed their families the most but loved the cabin. "Maybe we can arrange to come back next summer for a couple of weeks?"

They surfed the channels to catch other coverage of the incidents and realized one of the channels was covering their own area. They stopped and watched for the videos again but had to wait quite a while. When they finally showed the replay, all three gasped as they watched George's partners being led into FBI headquarters, followed by Gregory Marchman and several other people, including the mayor. This set the girls off into a whole other set of theories.

An FBI spokesman came to the front doors and asked everyone to go home. The excitement was over for the day and that no one would be saying anything until the following day. He set a press conference for ten a.m. the following day and went back inside. The press had their own theories and continued to show the videos of everyone being brought into the building in handcuffs.

The women continued to change channels and began watching the national news once again. There was a ruckus at the senator's offices and several other big-name people across the nation. It was when they started to discuss the shooting of Hank Elliott and agents on the scene that Edna became uneasy. The more they discussed it, the worse she felt. In her gut, she knew that James had been a casualty. Edna didn't want to say anything to the other women in case she was wrong.

"I'm headed for bed, girls. I've had all the excitement I can take today."

Martha was still riveted to the TV, but Sarah agreed to lock everything up and they would head to bed soon too. Edna went to her room. She thought back to what James had told her—no video in the bedrooms, just voice.

"James, if you hear me, we are fine. I hope you are. If you get this, just know that if you don't come back, we will find our way off the mountain safely." Edna turned in and had a very restless and sleepless night.

Two weeks later, the food was running low, and Edna's spirits were just as low. She knew it was time to figure out how to get off the mountain. Although she had considered several options, it was time to talk it out with the other women. None of them were spring chickens, but they were all healthy. The time on the mountain had forced outdoor exercise on them, and they all felt like they were in the best physical condition they had been in for years. The women were all sitting on the porch enjoying their morning cup of coffee. Edna finally spoke up.

"Girls, I think it's time to try to get these bracelets off or figure out how to dismantle the battery. In all of our walks, I have never seen the contraption that keeps the electronic barrier running, have you?" They both shook their heads. "Have either of you found a toolbox?" she asked. Sarah contemplated the kitchen area as Martha thought about the rest of the house.

Martha finally said, "You know, there is a shed out back that is locked up. I assumed it held a mower or something, but if we can get in there, we might be able to find some tools."

The women put down their cups and wandered to the back of the cabin. The shed was built of sturdy pine, and the hasp was fairly new. The hinges were such that they wouldn't be able to get to the screws.

"Someone knew what they were doing when they built this. There is no way to get into that thing without an ax, and I'm betting the ax is inside."

The women walked back into the house and decided

to see what they could find. After an hour-long search, there was nothing to be found that would resemble a tool. "We're going to have to figure out how to get out of here, you know," Edna said. The women's good moods decreased with the amount of food on hand. Something would have to give pretty soon.

******

John Peterson grew up in the big city and never felt like he fit in. When he was a child, his grandpa would take him fishing way up in the mountains every summer. His grandfather had a little cabin, and the two of them would fish for hours. They didn't even care if they didn't catch anything. Grandpa taught him the art of relaxing and napping by the shade of a tree with the stream running by. At first, John would play and splash in the stream, until he finally was old enough to know that if you scared the fish away, you wouldn't get to eat them either.

When he was a teenager, his grandfather suddenly passed away. When they settled the estate, his grandmother sold the cabin. She never liked the isolation of the cabin, and outside of his grandfather and himself, he was the only one who would miss it. Over time, he had gone fishing elsewhere, but the draw of the mountain cabin always made him wishful for the time with his grandfather. He wanted to share that with his own son someday.

The property had been sold twice since his grandfather died, and he couldn't find the name of the current owner. He wanted to go one more time before he moved across the country after accepting a job a thousand miles from home. He decided to go up to the mountain anyway, and hope for the best.

John drove toward the mountain and began to relax and anticipate fresh trout. When he pulled onto the curving access road, he was surprised to find a locked gate. He pulled off to the side of the road, parked, got out, and walked over to the gate. Frustrated, he looked around. There was no fence, just a gate. Feeling brave, he decided to gather his equipment and walk up the hill. He could hear the bubbling stream from where he was and decided to fish along the bank as he walked up the mountain.

Grabbing a large backpack and multiple other items, he headed toward the sounds of the stream. His plan all along was to camp out for a few days, but he hadn't planned on dragging his stuff on his back all the way up the mountain. *"If I'm going to trespass, I might as well do it big time."*

Making sure he had everything he needed, he locked the car and began hiking toward the stream and uphill at the same time. He left a note in his windshield that said he was by the stream somewhere, apologized for trespassing, and stated he wouldn't bother anyone. He had a gun packed away in case he needed to scare off a bear or cat. John began to whistle as he hiked, happy to be back on the mountain.

He spent the next three nights hiking up the mountain and fishing. He ate what he caught and only made a fire for cooking. He put it out with water from the stream. His grandfather taught him to never leave trash behind or a fire smoldering. He was never in a hurry and spent much of the time remembering the stories his grandfather told him.

By the fourth day, he traveled about as high as he could. The snow was almost gone, but the water was still running full force. He decided to get up on the boulders and look down on the mountain to see how far up he was.

It took a while to climb over the rocks and find a way to the top of an outcropping. As he surveyed the area, he was surprised to see a cabin not far from him. Looking around, he saw people out wandering in the yard and looking around. Finding no other cabin in the area, he decided that his grandfather's cabin had been torn down and a new one put up in its place. It was huge and hard to miss. He didn't blame the owners for rebuilding. By now, the little shanty would have been falling down anyway. It wasn't much when he had stayed in it all those years ago. It was no wonder his grandmother hated it. The old cabin had an outhouse and no running water. The current cabin looked as if it had everything you needed. He even saw the satellite for the TV. Chuckling, he carefully got down from the rocks and decided to stop by and introduce himself.

It took John over an hour to make his way to the cabin. He gathered up all his belongings first, pulled the stringer of fish, and decided to offer fresh fish to the new owners. He popped through the brush and walked toward the cabin. The women were all on the porch and gasped at the newcomer.

"Hello. I bring you the catch of the day." Edna jumped up.

"Where did you come from?"

John stopped in his tracks, not sure if he was welcomed or not. "I'm sorry to be trespassing. My name is

John Peterson, and I've been hiking up the mountain and fishing along the stream. I saw the cabin and thought you might like some fresh fish."

Edna's heart was pounding, and it was the first time she had panicked since coming to the mountain. She finally began to breathe deep and relax. The other women felt the same way and were murmuring to themselves behind her.

"Thank you for the fish. Come on up here and have a seat. Sarah, could you and Martha take the fish in and clean them? We'll fix them for lunch and have this fine young man join us."

The women hurriedly grabbed the fish and headed into the house, leaving Edna with the fisherman. He looked puzzled as the women went into the house and shut the door.

"Don't mind them. We've been up here all summer, and I think they forgot how to be friendly with strangers. Sit down here and tell me about yourself."

John dropped everything on the porch and sat with relief in one of the rockers. He looked out across the meadow, and it brought back memories. He smiled and looked over at Edna.

"I'm sorry to trespass. This property used to belong to my grandfather many years ago. I loved coming up here with him to fish. He started to bring me when I was just a little tadpole myself. After he died, my grandmother sold it, and I hadn't been here since. I'm moving across the country, and I had to see it one more time."

"It is beautiful up here. I don't blame you." They sat looking out at the scenery and rocking.

John finally broke the silence. "You've been up here all summer?"

"Most of it."

"You're lucky to own this. It's so peaceful."

"I don't own it. We're just staying here."

"Nice. Do you know who the owner is? I tried to contact them to get permission to come up, but I couldn't locate them."

"No. We arrived quite suddenly. Listen, why not get cleaned up for lunch? Leave your stuff right here on the porch and join us in the dining room. I'll show you around later."

John nodded and Edna took him in the house, showed him the bathroom and where the dining room was, and left him while she went into the kitchen. The two women had fish simmering, and Sarah had thrown together some hush puppies with the last of the cornmeal.

Edna saw everything was under control in the kitchen and said, "Let's hope this is our way out, girls. I don't want to say anything yet. We need to make sure he is as innocent as he looks." They both nodded and began getting everything ready to serve. Edna went to the dining room to visit with John while waiting for the final touches on lunch.

"You'll enjoy Sarah's cooking. She can whip

something together out of nothing. We even put up jam while here. We made them from the berries up the hill. She was bound and determined to beat the bears to them." The two visited while Edna showed John the main floor. "I'll show you around outside before you go."

Lunch was magnificent, and John polished off most of the hush puppies by himself. "I hadn't realized how hungry I was. I'm sorry to make such a pig of myself, but it was all so delicious."

Sarah thanked him. "Where are you going from here?"

"I'll head back down the hill and then home. I'm a little overdue now. It was so nice up here, I couldn't stop fishing. It made new memories for me."

Edna looked at the other women, and they both gave her a slight nod. "Would you do us a favor when you get to the city?"

"Sure. What do you need?"

"You see, we have no cell phone coverage and the landline hasn't been put in yet. Could you get a hold of my nephew for me and tell him we are ready to come home now? He wasn't coming back for a few more weeks, but since you are here, if you would give him the message from us we would certainly appreciate it."

"Sure, just let me know who to contact."

Martha jumped up and went to get a paper and pencil. Edna chuckled nervously at Martha's over exuberance. "I think Martha is more than ready to go home."

John laughed. Edna took the paper and pencil from Martha and thought for a bit. "My, oh my. I can't remember his number. You know how it is. Things are programmed into your cell phones and you never dial numbers anymore.

This is his name." She wrote Tom Edwards's name down. "I'm so proud of my nephew. He works for the FBI and is a hotshot for them. You can just go to his office downtown and find him."

"I know that name. Let's see, wasn't he involved in that big sweep of extortionists the other day?"

"I'm sure he was. Hopefully, he can see his way clear to come up and get us anyway. I'm sorry. I better put my name on this paper so you remember it." She wrote her name and handed the paper to him. "One more thing, young man."

"Yes, ma'am."

"Tell him we need some bolt cutters."

"Bolt cutters?" Edna smiled. "Yes. It seems that we have locked ourselves out of something."

John smiled back. "All right. If you don't mind, I'll hike the road back down the hill. It will be easier and faster for me."

"No problem. Drive safely, and it was nice to meet you. Maybe you can return here someday."

"I hope to. If you find out who the owners are, put in a good word for me, will you?" John handed them a piece of paper with his own name and number.

"Absolutely." They watched as John loaded up his pack and headed down the long and winding road.

It would be the following day before he would be able to contact Tom, but they felt help would be on the way soon. The women talked excitedly and decided to get the cabin cleaned up and their clothes packed in anticipation of being able to leave.

Edna and Martha spent the rest of the day washing

clothes and cleaning the cabin while Sarah looked over the last of the food supplies and made sure to freeze anything that could spoil. There were only a few days left of their supply and hoped that they would be rescued before the food ran out. They were putting all their hopes on John Peterson.

The women watched the news that evening and didn't learn anything new about the arrests. It was becoming old news by then, and there was very little coverage. They talked about being able to go home again, and the women were planning on seeing their family first before returning to the Chessmore estate. Edna reassured them that they could have as much time as they wanted, and to arrive back to work whenever they were ready. She told them they could even take the rest of the summer off if they wanted to. The women agreed to think about it and would decide once they were home. None of them slept well that night in anticipation of being rescued the following day. They had breakfast and sat on the porch like usual, having their coffee. No one talked, and everyone listened for any signs of a rescue.

Edna finally said, "This is silly. It's so early in the morning that there is no way anyone will be here this soon. Let's just go about our normal business. John might not even find Tom, or Tom might not be around what with all that other nonsense going on."

The women agreed, and they cleaned up the breakfast mess and spent some time wandering the grounds. Edna tested her bracelet, and it was still active so she backed off. The other women did the same and decided it was too risky to try to walk through the perimeter.

Sarah sighed at the prospect of fixing lunch. "I was hoping to be home by now."

Edna patted her on the shoulder, then fixed a few sandwiches. None of them were very hungry but ate out of habit. Sarah cleaned everything up in anticipation of leaving once again, and all of their clothes were packed into the sacks and boxes that James had brought their groceries in. They sat on the porch hoping to watch their rescue arrive that afternoon.

The sun was beginning to drop behind the mountain before they thought they could hear someone coming up the road. Before long, the noise became quite loud as three vehicles came screaming up the drive and up to the cabin. The men all jumped out and came running as the women rose from their chairs, crying as their rescue finally arrived.

Tom was first to arrive. "Are you ladies all right? Are you hurt? Why do you need bolt cutters?"

The women looked at each other, and through tears, cracked up laughing. Their nerves were so taut that they couldn't stop laughing or crying. The men stood looking at each other like the women lost their minds. Tom just shrugged at the men and mouthed, *"Women."* Edna finally contained herself and held out her wrist. She hiccupped from the crying and laughing and explained they needed to have the bracelets cut off before they could leave as they would shock them otherwise. All the women held out their arms and showed the men their bracelets.

"I see."

He nodded at someone to bring over the bolt cutters, and once they had the women rest their arms on the railing, the agent managed to cut the band off without hurting them very much. The agent took one and jogged to the side yard for several yards. They finally heard him yelp in pain.

The women laughed, and together they said, "We told you." This made them laugh harder.

The men gathered up all the women's clothes and items and put them in one of the vehicles. They all wanted to ride together, and Tom decided to take their statement as they went back down the mountain. He was surprised to find out that James had taken them into seclusion and more than surprised they had been fine all this time. It was a relief to everyone involved.

Once he got as many details as he could, Edna asked him. "You weren't too hard on that young man that found us, were you?"

Tom looked sheepish. "I might have been. He looked pretty distraught when I began to interrogate him. When we looked at his phone and saw all the new fishing pictures and scenery, I decided to believe him. He was probably relieved by then."

"The poor boy. I'll have to call him and thank him for

his trouble. By the way, I need to know something. Did James get hurt in the raid?"

"I'll have to get back to you on that. I'm not sure what I can tell you at this point. We are still sorting everything out. Right now, I think we will just get you women home."

The women agreed that it was highest thing on their agenda, too. Tom looked out the windshield as their driver headed into the city. He really didn't know what to tell Mrs. Chessmore about James, even if he knew the answer. He planned to find out as soon as they got back into the office the following day.

The FBI cars pulled up to the gate of the Chessmore estate and buzzed. Mike asked who was there, and Tom let him know he and some friends arrived. Mike let them through and met them at the front door. As everyone got out of the car, he couldn't believe his eyes.

"Mrs. Chessmore? Martha? Sarah? You're home. Tom, where did you find them? Are you women all okay?" Mike ran over and gave each one a hug.

The women chuckled and hugged him back. "Let's go inside, Mike. I'll tell you everything, but Martha and Sarah want to go home first."

He grabbed them again and Tom shook his hand. "Take care of her this time."

Mike looked a little embarrassed at the remark and led Mrs. Chessmore into the house. Tom unloaded Edna's items, and the other two women got back into the car for home. Tom informed them they must keep to the story that they were on a long vacation with their boss. The two felt they really had been, so it wouldn't be far from the truth. They were both well rested but ready to get back to their families. Mike led Mrs. Chessmore back inside and brought her to the office. She stopped in shock to see her lovely den changed into a functional office.

"What is going on around here?"

Mike led her over to the wingback chairs that still sat by the windows. "I think we both have things to talk about, but first, tell me, how you are? Were you hurt? How did the ladies end up with you? How did Tom find you?"

"Slow down, Mike. Let me get my breath." Edna looked around and actually liked the looks of the new office but didn't say anything yet. She looked back at Mike who sat on the edge of his seat, waiting for her to talk about her summer. "When I left the office, I came down the elevator as usual and knew you were waiting for me. About the time I walked in front of the main doors, someone grabbed me and shoved me into a car. I was blindfolded and gagged with a rag that had something on it that knocked me out. The first twenty-four hours were pretty scary because the man that took me was nasty, and he had a really sharp knife. Then I was transported to a cabin high up in the mountains and left there. I had a bracelet on that would zap me if I went too far from the perimeter of the cabin. Otherwise, I was fine. It was a beautiful place. A week later, Martha and Sarah were brought by and dropped off. We spent the summer up there, hiking and wandering around and having a good time. It was actually very healing. The man that took us there turned out to be someone that hid us all for our own safety. It's too bad he didn't tell you, but he didn't tell anyone."

Edna caught her breath. "Yesterday, we had a fisherman stop by and offered us some fish. We asked him to contact Tom, and here we are."

"Amazing. I was so scared you were in trouble or dead. I've been feeling guilty all this time."

"With me gone, why did you decide to stay here? Not that's a problem or anything."

"Yeah, well. Here's the thing. Once you didn't come back and then the other women disappeared, there were still people watching the place like you were still here. I drove back and forth to the office every day just as if you were living here, and it was driving me crazy. Then I decided I would do like you wanted to do to begin with and moved your staff to the other branches and hauled Janda here to run the office from your home. I was hoping you wouldn't mind that I did all that. When the FBI still couldn't find you, I had the board designate a temporary CEO while you were gone so the business could function. Mrs. Whethers has been handling all of that and is doing a fine job, I believe."

Edna looked around again. "I like the way it's set up. It fits nicely in here."

"Janda actually directed where to put everything. She runs this place like a well-oiled machine."

"What about my embezzlement issue? Did anyone figure that out?"

"It was Bradley Jenkins."

"What?"

"I just found out the other day, but my understanding is that he paid you back. Doris is out of jail now, and Tom checked on her whereabouts. She is working with Bradley at a private optometry office. Bradley had to sell everything to pay all his debts. He had been gambling it all away."

"Good lord. What else did I miss out on?"

"Janda is doing an excellent job, but she will be thrilled to find you back home when she arrives tomorrow."

"I bet." Edna looked around. "So. What have you been up to since I've been gone?"

"Well, I was going to move back to my apartment, but Janda didn't want to be here by herself. It's a good thing. She's had some nasty visitors while you were gone."

"Like who?"

"Mr. Marchman, Steve Perry, and Max."

"I can understand Max coming by, but why the other two?"

"They wanted you and some file. I had to get pretty firm with all of them, and Janda actually had to call the police on Mr. Marchman."

"Oh my. The poor thing. The file. Hmmm. Evidently, there was a file I should have known about. That was one of the reasons I was tucked away. I didn't know anything about it, and James thought he needed to keep me safe because of it."

"James?"

"Yes, the man that hid us away. I'm afraid he got hurt or killed in the big shootout in Washington, but I haven't heard anything since. That was why we had the fishermen tell Tom to come get us. James told me only two people knew where we were, and since it had been a couple of weeks, we figured they were both hurt really bad or killed. It's just a hunch that he was involved in it somehow, but Tom said he would try to find out for me. James told me he had to finish the mission, so I put two and two together."

"I'll go fix you a hot tea. Are you hungry?"

"A light snack would be fine. I'll walk with you. I need to see my house again."

They both walked to the kitchen, and Mike proceeded to make them both some tea and sandwiches. They sat at the counter, and Edna looked toward the patio door.

"The roses?"

"They are beautiful. I've kept them watered, but the gardener quit a couple of weeks ago. The company said they would send someone else to replace him, but they haven't yet. Now that you're home, I can do it. I just didn't want to leave Janda alone in here. I picked up a few odd jobs while you were gone and needed the weekends to catch up on my own projects."

Edna sighed. "Thank you for keeping things going for me. I never even worried about the company while I was gone. Maybe I better sell out since I seem to have lost all interest in everything I used to hold dear."

"Whatever you want to do, Mrs. Chessmore. But in the meantime, how about we take a stroll through the roses?"

"What a lovely idea, Mike. You need to start calling me Edna. All my friends call me Edna, and I consider you a good friend. I finally got Martha and Sarah to stop calling me Mrs. Chessmore. I hope they don't start in again now that we are home."

Mike took her arm and led her out to the garden. They quietly walked in the rose garden, arm in arm, until Edna got her fill.

"Thank you, Mike. I believe I will head up to my room and retire for the night. We will have to discuss your job description tomorrow."

"Just so you know, I haven't billed you a dime since you were abducted. I have bought all my own food, and the only thing I've used on your property is my suite and your workout room. It will only take me a few minutes to pack my bags."

"No. Don't leave. That's not what I meant. I guess I don't know what I meant. We'll discuss it tomorrow."

"Sure. Good night, Edna."

She smiled and headed up the stairs for her own suite. It was good to be home. The following day, Janda arrived for work and found Mrs. Chessmore sitting at her own desk looking through stacks of files.

"Mrs. Chessmore. I'm so happy to see you again."

Edna got up and walked over to her and took her hands. "It's good to be home. Thank you so much for taking care of everything. I hear you have done an excellent job."

Janda blushed. "Thank you. I've really enjoyed learning about your company. Mrs. Whethers has helped me a lot."

"Mrs. Whethers, huh? Well, I will have to thank her profusely."

"She will be here later today to sign checks."

"Lovely. Well, let's get to work and see what I've missed out on. Seems like I just went through this same thing a few months ago, and I hope I don't find any surprises this time."

Even though Janda wanted to ask where her boss had been the last several weeks, she figured that subject could come up another time. Right now, she knew she needed to get down to business. She showed her boss what she had been doing while Edna was away. Her boss was grateful that everything was in order and said so. Edna looked at the financials and could see they were exceptionally clean and was grateful that Carson Shoemaker had remained involved.

When lunchtime rolled around, Edna sat back and smiled at Janda. "You don't need me, you need a raise. I'll send your new wage notification over to the HR office and include a bonus for keeping my company afloat."

"Thank you, but that isn't necessary. I love my job, and I try to do my best."

"Nonsense, my dear. You may not realize the impact you have made, but I have." Edna sat down and filled out her paperwork and faxed it right over to the HR office. "Done. Now you are my new corporate manager, with a wage to match. Now let's do lunch." Janda's jaw dropped.

Upon that announcement, Mike arrived. "Did someone say lunch?"

That afternoon, Mrs. Peggy Whethers arrived, and Edna and her good friend sat out on the back patio and visited at length. Edna had Janda join them while she explained the story of her adventures the last few months. Janda went back to work, in awe of her boss. Peggy remained to discuss the business, and Edna convinced Peggy to remain as the CEO of the company until she could make up her mind about selling or not.

"I need some time to decide, and you and Janda have handled everything just fine. Let's bring it up at the next meeting and see what the board thinks. The financials are solid, so this may be a good time to sell off." They hugged before Peggy left and agreed to stay in touch and discuss everything at the next meeting.

After Janda left for the day, Mike and Edna sat at the kitchen table enjoying some tea. "We really need to discuss your job description."

"I really don't have a job anymore. You are back and presumably safe now. I didn't keep you safe to begin with, so I'm not sure what benefit I can be. By the way, I haven't given you all of the codes. I had to change everything once I found out people were walking around in here because they knew the codes. I didn't even give it to Janda. Now that you are back, I'll let you decide what to do with them. I also changed the safe combination because someone had that too."

"The safe? Someone got into the safe?"

"Evidently. There was a break-in, and Jordan and I caught them before they could take anything because they triggered several of the silent alarms. Believe it or not, they had the combination to the safe. When I looked at the tape, I noticed someone had come in without setting off the alarms, disconnected the video feed for a short time, and then turned it back on before leaving and rearming the alarms. Tom, Jordan, and I got into the safe, but there wasn't anything special in there. But I reset the combination anyway because of the significant amount of cash."

Edna was listening intently. "I think that was where George had a file that everyone wanted, but you say there wasn't anything in there?"

"Not much. Let me get the numbers, and we'll get in there for you to see."

Mike had written them all down on a small notepad and secreted them until Edna came home. He dug it out and met Edna in the hallway. They walked to the office, and Mike took the picture down. Edna worked the new combination and opened the safe. She took out the passports and a few other items, put the money aside, and felt around.

"You're right. There is nothing much in there." Edna puzzled over the safe as she placed her items back inside. She took a quick count of money and realized her husband had tucked a significant amount away. "I wonder why he had so much cash in here? I'll need to get that to the bank. Everything he did those last few months was so troubling. Maybe he thought the partners would bring him down with them and wanted to make sure he wasn't completely broke."
"That would make sense. Do you have any idea who would have taken the file if it was in there?"
"James. I think James took it. Not that I know that for sure, but he asked me some very specific questions about George. I wonder if George gave him the file or gave him the combination to the safe. It's all so confusing."
"We may never know, but either way, I'm glad he kept you safe."
Edna turned and smiled. "Me, too." They closed up the safe and hung the picture back up. Edna tucked the notebook in her pocket. "Let's go out for supper, my treat. But you can drive me." They both laughed and headed for the car.
"You still haven't told me what my job description

is."

"Tonight, you are my driver. Tomorrow, who knows? All I know is that I have come to depend on you, and I really don't want you to leave."

They headed down the street, and Mike drove straight to her favorite place downtown a few blocks from her old office. The owners were thrilled to see her once again and led them to her favorite table. Mike and Edna had a wonderful evening, and got to know each other better. They never had time for personal conversation before, and they found they had many things in common, especially Edna's choices in restaurants.

Edna, full from one of her favorite meals, sat back and sipped her coffee. "Tomorrow I suppose I better call Max."

Mike grimaced. "He will be thrilled to hear from you."

Edna saw the look on Mike's face. "You don't like him much, do you?"

"Let's just say he isn't one of my favorite people. He is pretty condescending, and Janda has no use for his cocky attitude. I had to throw him out while you were gone, so I'm sure he will have something to say about us."

"Don't worry about it. I've known Max a long time. He and his wife were good friends, but Max is a spoiled brat. I just ignore him."

Mike nodded and tried to keep his opinions to himself. As they drove home, he looked over to Edna and said, "If Max gets out of line with you or Janda, I won't sit by and let it happen."

Edna chuckled. "I guess we can add bouncer to your list of jobs." Mike grinned and drove home.

Dutifully, Edna called Max the following morning and invited him over for brunch. Max jumped in his car and headed straight over. Janda asked if it would be all right to keep the office doors closed during his visit, and Edna agreed without question. Since Mike's revelation from the night before, she didn't question Janda as to why. Mike offered to fix their meal and serve it, and they decided to put butler and cook on his job duties. Max was buzzed in, and Edna met him at the door. Max grabbed her and hugged her tight and barraged her with questions as she led him to the patio. She had Max sit down, and she poured him some coffee.

Sitting across from him she said, "Catch your breath. I'll tell you all about my vacation once we are served."

Shortly, Mike came out with a serving cart and provided their brunch. Edna told him that she would serve the meal, and Mike went back in the house. Max was livid that Mike was still in the house and immediately complained to Edna.

"And another thing. That new secretary of yours is a real piece of work. You need to fire her and get Doris back. I was treated just awful by both of those idiots."

Edna sighed. "I thought you came over to see me and hear about my vacation."

"I did, but you don't know how I was so rudely

treated while you were gone."

"Get over it and eat your meal. I'm starved."

Edna dug into her breakfast and enjoyed every bite while Max sat there sulking. He eventually ate, and when he was done, he complimented Sarah's meal.

"Mike cooked it." That set Max off once again and wondered where Sarah and Martha were.

"I let them go visit their family for a few weeks. Why are you so worried about my staff anyway?"

"I just think that we need to make sure we have the right staff in place."

"We? What are you talking about?"

"I thought you knew how I felt about you and that we would eventually get together, travel, and enjoy life, you know?"

Edna put her napkin on the table, her mouth gaping at his words. "You thought you and I would get married?"

"Yes. Don't you think that is the perfect solution?"

"Solution to what?"

"We are both alone, and we've been good friends. I figured you could sell everything, and we could travel all over the world."

"I see. Travel as in on my money."

Max looked away as he answered. "Yes, I guess so. I mean, you have so much more than I do."

"Well. I hadn't really thought about it like that. I can see how it would benefit you in the long run."

"I'm glad you see it my way. That's why we need to get rid of these incompetent servants of yours and hire people who know their place."

"Actually, Max, I believe it is you who doesn't know

your place. Let's go."

"Where are we going?"

"We aren't going anywhere except to the door. You are leaving."

Max blustered. "Why?"

Edna took his elbow and led him toward the front door. "First of all, we are not getting married. Second of all, you are not getting a dime from me. Third, when you decide to be civil to my staff, you can come back but not before. I've appreciated your friendship for years, but you need to decide if my friendship is worth it or not. Goodbye, Max." Edna shut the door on his surprised face, turned, and leaned back on the door. "*What an idiot,*" she murmured.

Mike was cleaning up the dishes when Edna came back out to the patio. "I enjoyed the meal, Mike. You are quite the cook. Even Max enjoyed it until I told him you cooked it."

They both laughed, and Edna helped him finish cleaning up. He took the cart back inside and left Edna wandering the grounds. He knew she needed to feel at home once again and enjoy her freedom. He had just finished loading the dishwasher when she came back into the kitchen.

He turned to her. "Do you want some tea?"
"Sure."

He went to work and fixed them a pot. They sat in silence while enjoying the tea. Edna was looking through the patio doors. "A lot can happen in a split second. One second you are enjoying a meal and the next you are throwing one of your best friends out the door." Mike looked surprised. "You were right. He is a condescending fool."

"I never called him a fool."

"Right, you didn't, but you shouldn't have any more problems with him."

Mike nodded and finished his tea. "I need to go to my apartment and water the plants and get my mail."

Edna looked at him. "Move in here."

Mike paused. "And?"

"I don't know, but I don't want you to move out."

Mike looked thoughtfully at Edna. "I'll think about it."

******

Tom and his fellow agents finished all their investigation and paperwork, and time would tell how everything played out through the justice system. The jails across the country were full of men and women the FBI and police picked up, and several of the people hired to watch Edna and run errands finally talked since their bosses were sitting behind bars.

Mark Lincoln requested not to be in the same cell as his partners and spent several hours over the first few days telling everything he knew about their part in the scams they were running. Unlike George, who refused to be involved, he tried to stay out of it for a while, but the money sounded too good to be true. Once they became involved with Gregory Marchman and began covering his business entities, they were caught.

Business opportunities became money laundering schemes. Then it stretched into embezzlement from big corporations by involving senators, mayors, governors, and other high-ranking officials. Edna Chessmore was caught in the middle because George Chessmore held a file on everything they had been doing, and they wanted it back. That was the last straw for Mark Lincoln. There was no way out and no way to win. Mark would be a key witness for the FBI in the future and made sure he cleared George's name in the process. He didn't want to hurt Edna any more.

The charges varied from embezzlement, money laundering, taking bribes, and racketeering to running a betting entity. No matter the position, someone was being threatened by another authority figure. By the time the senators were involved, federal money was being designated for state causes that didn't even exist. There was money flowing from every direction. With Hank Elliot and many of his gang out of the way, it was only a matter of time before someone else started the cycle over again.

Tom called Dave and asked about James. The details were sketchy, and Dave wasn't at liberty to talk about it right then. All Dave could tell him was that he was alive but it was touch and go and they wouldn't know for some time. He had no idea what to tell Mrs. Chessmore, so he didn't tell her anything.

The local mayor resigned in shame and he agreed to be a witness against Gregory Marchman. Every time Gregory wanted something, a little money went his way to make sure it happened quickly. His wife of many years hid her head in shame, moved out of town, and wanted to file for a divorce. The man she married had let her down, and she couldn't live with the cloud hanging over her head. She loved the extra money coming in but never asked where he was getting it from. She had been a snob to so many people once her husband got into office, and now she was the one being shunned. He begged her to forgive him and try to work things out, but she wasn't sure she could. He was more devastated that his marriage was in shambles than the possibility of him going to jail.

Bradley Jenkins was able to see Gregory Marchman and offered to buy the chain of optometry shops back from him for ten cents on the dollar. Since he had been running the businesses into the ground, they now had a bad name. Gregory knew that he would probably never see the light of day again, and the judge refused to let him bail out of jail. Now he needed the cash up front for the lawyers, so he countered Bradley's offer for twenty cents on the dollar. Bradley agreed and had Mr. Popoff draw up the paperwork. Bradley made a deal for his new boss and agreed to help him get the corporation all back on track, but he didn't want to run it himself. It was time for new blood to take the reins and build up the business once again. He agreed to remain a silent partner and was adamant about only owning twenty-five percent of the business.

******

The leaves were starting to turn before Mike took Edna up on the offer to move completely out of his apartment and into her house. He closed up the apartment the month before and she gave him an additional room to set up all of his electronic equipment. He worked out a schedule for monitoring his own security business and helping Edna around the house. They spent a lot of time together walking the grounds and watching the last of the rose petals drop off.

Martha and Sarah came back after the Labor Day holiday and went right to work like they had never been gone. Martha's only comment was that Mike wasn't the best at housekeeping, and Mike pretended to be offended. The women agreed to continue to use Edna's first name unless she was entertaining. Once they returned, Edna felt like her life had finally gotten back on track.

At the last board meeting, she discussed the possibility of selling, and the board agreed the time was perfect as each entity was doing well. She was going to have to decide what to do next, and Mike encouraged her to relax through the holidays and wait until the first of the year to make that decision.

Tom finally called Edna about James. He had put it off long enough and promised her an answer. All he knew was that the injuries were serious and he was fighting for his life. It was this type of news he hated delivering. Tom asked Dave to make sure that James knew Edna, Martha, and Sarah were all safe. Edna didn't feel much better when she finally knew his condition because now she was worried about him being so ill. She finally discussed it with Mike.

"He did everything to protect me. I just feel like I should do something to help him."

Mike thought about it for a while. "How about I take you to him? We'll see if Tom can find out where he is, and then we will fly out there and thank him for a job well done. What do you say?"

"That would be perfect. Do you think they will let us in to see him?"

"I hope so. It would relieve your mind, I think."

She thought for a moment. "Yes. Let's see if you can find out where he is. Can you get away for a while?"

"I can call Jordan to stay here and monitor things for

me. He's done it before."

"Let's do it."

It was a couple of days before Tom got back to Mike about James's whereabouts, but he finally gave him a call. "I had to wait for someone to give you the green light to see him. I was told to let Mrs. Chessmore know that he looks rough, but James is ready to see her."

"Good. We'll fly out tomorrow. Just let them know we are on the way and expect us tomorrow or the next day, depending on the flights we catch."

"Will do."

"Tom?"

"Yeah?"

"Thanks. This means a lot to Edna."

"You don't know the half of it, buddy."

With that, Tom hung up and left Mike wondering what he was talking about. He let Edna know they could visit, and Mike made the reservations to fly into Washington the following afternoon. It would be too late to go to the hospital by the time they got to the hotel, so they planned to go over first thing the following morning.

They each got settled into their rooms and met in the lobby to find a place for supper. They ate supper, and Edna contemplated what she would find the following day. Mike was still mulling over Tom's comment and had his own worries. Each one retired for the night knowing that they wouldn't be getting a restful night, each for their own reasons.

The hotel was only a couple of blocks from the hospital, so they chose to walk over. The morning was crisp, the leaves were turning, and the traffic was crazy. Mike took Edna's arm as they carefully made their way to the entrance of the hospital and found the elevators to the fourth floor. Once there, Edna told a nurse who she was and that she was expected to see James.

"Mrs. Chessmore, come right this way. We were expecting you. Did you have a nice flight?"

"Yes, thank you." The nurse led them to the end of the hall and pointed to a door. "You may go in, Mrs. Chessmore. Sir, I don't have clearance for you right now. It will be up to the patient whether or not you may go in."

"That's fine. Edna, you go on in. If you need me, I'll be right here."

The nurse nodded at them and left. Edna took a deep breath and opened the door to find a dimly lit room and someone covered head to toe in bandages and tubes.

As she walked in, she said, "James? It's Edna. Edna Chessmore."

"Good morning. Pull up a chair and have a seat. I'm glad you're here," he croaked out. Edna pulled a chair close and reached for his hand. He held it tight and took a deep breath. "How did you get off the mountain?"

"A fisherman found us, and I sent word to someone to come get us. I heard on the news about the shootout, and somehow I knew you were involved. No one told me anything for a long time."

James continued to hold her hand and a tear rolled

down his face. "I didn't want you to know in case I died. It would be too much for you to bear."

"What are you talking about?"

He let go of her hand and reached over to turn on a brighter light. Once they were both used to the brighter light, James said, "Stand up and come closer."

Edna got up and moved closer to the bed. James reached up and touched Edna's face. "It's good to see you again, Mom." Edna stood there in shock and then screamed. Mike heard the scream and came tearing into the room.

"What is it? Edna, are you all right?" Edna stood there shaking and finally sat back down in her chair. She was blubbering by then and unable to talk. "What's going on? What did you do to her?" Mike said.

Edna shook her head, and James had a slight smile on his face. "It's good to finally meet you in person, Mike. Thanks for taking care of my mother."

Mike looked like someone slapped him. "I don't get it. What is going on around here?"

Edna finally got herself under control. "I don't know what is going on, but this is my son. I thought I lost him a long time ago and here he is, and I almost lost him again."

James reached out to his mother. "It's time to explain everything."

Mike stepped up. "You better, young man. This is no joking matter."

James nodded, and Edna grabbed his hand and held on with one hand and wiped her eyes with the other. Mike stood behind her with his hands on her shoulders for support. He gathered his thoughts and took a long drink of water.

"Mom, you knew I was working for the government when I was supposedly killed." She nodded. "The man that shot me was Hank Elliot. He thought I was dead, and we decided I needed to stay that way. Technically, they did have to bring me back once, so it was pretty close to being true. I lost a lot of blood by the time my partners found me. I decided to go underground and work to get this guy, but in order to do that, I had to let you go through with the funeral and everything. I've kept an eye on you ever since, but I couldn't let you know I was alive." He stopped for another drink of water. "I didn't know it at the time, but Dad stumbled onto some of the same information I was tracking. The problem was, he didn't turn the file over before he died. He called our office, and we were just starting to investigate it when he had his heart attack. I was devastated. I attended the funeral and saw what a mess you were, but I couldn't do anything to offer support at the time. I remembered the combination of the safe and walked in one night to get the file. Dad told my partner where he kept it. You may not believe this, but I was your gardener for a while. It was an easy cover, and it helped me keep track of what was going on. I found out later from Tom Edwards that you had several other things going on at the same time. I felt helpless, but all I knew was that I had to keep you safe and make sure I got back home to you."

Edna had been listening quietly, sobbing occasionally, and still reeling from shock from the news that this was her son in front of her.

"Anyway, we went back in to arrest Hank Elliot, and when my supervisor was killed outside the building, I took my eyes off of Hank for a second, and he took the opportunity to shoot me again. This time, he almost got it done. Even though I had my vest on, he managed to catch me in a few places it didn't cover, and one grazed my head. My last thought was trying to tell someone about you being on the mountaintop, but I blacked out. By the time I was lucid enough to ask, I found out you had been rescued. I was so relieved, but I still wasn't sure I would live. I was going to come home once I was discharged from the hospital, but when they said you wanted to come, I was grateful to see you and said yes immediately." He turned to Mike. "Thanks for bringing her."

Mike nodded, not knowing what else to say. He decided to leave the two of them alone to visit and went out into the hall. He shook his head at the news and walked down the hall to find something to drink. He knew Edna would need something to drink by now, too. He found a little kitchenette for guests and fixed her some hot tea and grabbed two bottles of water. He walked back to the room, carefully came through the door, and sat her drinks beside her. He encouraged her to drink her tea while it was hot. James was evidently sleeping, but Edna continued to hold his hand. Mike said he would be back later and pointed at the tea. She smiled and promised to drink it.

He left the room and headed outdoors to wander the streets for a restaurant that would be perfect for Edna. By the time he found one and walked back to the room, it had been almost two hours. Edna was dozing next to James, still holding his hand. He tapped her shoulder to wake her. She looked around, smiled, and stood up. Leaning over James, she kissed him on his forehead, and they left the room. She told the nurse she would return after lunch, and they left the hospital. Mike took Edna's hand and led her down the street to the quaint restaurant he almost missed in his earlier trek.

They ate, talked little, and Edna spent the time mulling over her recent visit. Mike walked her back to the hospital room, and he promised to come get her later in the afternoon. When he arrived, James and Edna were reminiscing and laughing about some hijinks James did when he was small. Mike could tell James was exhausted and promised to bring Edna back the following morning. It was all Edna could do to leave him for the night, but Mike reassured her that she could leave her number at the nurse's stations if they needed her.

They agreed neither one was hungry enough to stop for supper. When they got in front of the hotel doors, Mike asked if she wanted him to knock on her door and get her in the morning for breakfast or just meet her downstairs. She stated she wanted him to stop and get her first. The next day after breakfast, Mike walked Edna back to the hospital room and told her he would be back just before lunch. He went back to the hotel to use the exercise room and burn off some energy.

Once he was cleaned up, he packed his bags for the return trip back home. Walking into the hospital room, he found Edna sound asleep on James's chest. He walked back out and waited for a nurse to wake them. He gave them a few minutes then returned to the room. He found Edna standing at the end of the bed watching the nurse take vitals and assess James.

"Are you ready to catch a plane home, Edna?"

"No. I can't leave now. I just got my baby back."

James looked at his mother and then at Mike. "Mike, take Mom home for now. I start therapy this afternoon, and it will be a gruesome sight for a while. Mom, please go home. Come back in a week and stay a couple of days. I'll be better by then once I've started therapy."

"I can't leave now that I have you back. What if something happens to you again?"

"It won't. Please, Mom, do this for me. Go home with Mike and let him take care of you now."

Edna looked over at Mike and back to James. "He has been, son, but I just got you back. How can you ask me to leave?"

"I'll be home before you know it. You can't stay. It will be too hard on both of us. I'll want to put on a brave face in therapy instead of bawl my eyes out."

Mike went over and gently took her hands. "Come on. You can fly back next week."

Edna walked over to James. "Are you sure I can't stay, son?"

"Yes, please go home. I love you, but I need the rest between therapy sessions."

She leaned over him and gave him a long hug and tried not to hurt him. She kissed his forehead, smoothed his hair, and said, "I love you, Xavier James. I'll see you next week."

They both had tears in their eyes, and Edna walked out the door with Mike right behind her. He turned and looked at James just as he was shutting the door. James mouthed "Thank you" as the door shut.

Mike helped Edna pack, and they caught a taxi back to the airport. They were soon on their way home. Edna had tears in her eyes most of the time, and Mike sat holding her hand for support. Once home, Edna went right up to her suite, and Mike brought her luggage up to her. He left it just inside the door and headed back downstairs. Martha and Sarah watched Edna struggle up the stairs and asked Mike what the problem was. He led them into the kitchen to explain about James. They, too, were shocked at who James turned out to be.

"It's no wonder he treated us like we were all special people, and it makes complete sense that he didn't want Edna to see him when he brought our groceries to us."

They were amazed at the revelation and promised to give her time and space to get used to the idea her son was alive.

Edna began a new schedule. She flew to Washington almost weekly for about a month. When James was moved to a rehabilitation center, he asked her to not come as often as he would be going through a tougher regimen and knew he would be tired. It was difficult for her, but she arranged to see him every two to three weeks, depending on the weather.

In the meantime, Janda organized a schedule for her boss in the office so she could handle her meetings with all of her retirement centers through Skype instead of having to travel. At first, she had several meetings every day to catch up on what was happening and help solve problems. Her facilities handled the change to Skype easily and felt they could have immediate access to her if needed. Edna apologized to each and every one of them for being an absentee owner in the past year and resolved to help make it up to them.

Edna, Janda, and Peggy Whethers decided to give each and every manager a bonus that year at Christmas because they had done such a great job keeping each place running without any major issues. Edna continued to be on the fence about selling out and decided that Mike's idea to wait until after the holidays to make any formal decision was sound. She continued to worry about James, although he was recovering quickly now that he was able to get up and around. His determination to get back to a hundred percent was evident in his hard work in rehab each day.

The weather was turning cold and blustery. James called and told her a front was moving in and the east coast was going to get hammered over Thanksgiving. He encouraged her to have a quiet dinner at home and he would see her soon. She was devastated she couldn't spend the holiday with him, but she also didn't want to get stuck sitting in an airport.

Sarah promised to have everything ready and packed in the refrigerator for Edna and Mike. Mike agreed to put everything together for their meal, and Sarah gave him lengthy instructions.

"If you have any questions, you just call me."
"We will be just fine. Even if I burn the meal, I'm not

calling you."

Sarah slapped him on the shoulder and headed home to her family. Martha had left a few days earlier, and the house seemed empty again. Edna even gave Janda the week off for the holiday.

Thanksgiving morning, Mike was busy in the kitchen, and Edna was standing in the office looking out her window at the leaves blowing around the yard. The day was gray and overcast, and she could see spits of moisture hit the window. She hadn't listened to the forecast, but her mood matched the weather outside. Mike brought them both some hot tea, and they stood there watching the wind blowing through the trees. It was becoming nastier as the day progressed.

"I better go check on dinner. Sarah will have a fit if I ruin it."

Edna chuckled as he walked away. She turned, looked around, and decided to sit at her desk to see if there was anything she could do while waiting for dinner. It was definitely too nasty to go outside for a walk. Just as she was starting to read a report, someone buzzed the gate. She went over to the camera to see who it was but didn't recognize the car. She opened the gate and waited at the door. Mike joined her, and waited for their guest to arrive. When they heard the car door slam, Edna opened the door and watched a figure hunched into his coat approach the doorway.

It only took a second for Edna to exclaim, "James." He rushed into her open arms and picked her up, twirling her into the air. "Put me down right now, young man. You're going to hurt yourself." James laughed, and they all went back inside the toasty house. "What are you doing here?" Edna asked.

"I'm dismissed and home to stay," James said.

"Home to stay? Do you mean it? What about your job?"

"Being on my deathbed twice in just a few years is enough for me. I'm done. I turned in my resignation, and as the first of December I'll be a free agent. Are you hiring?"

Edna grabbed him and held him tight. Mike sneaked back to the kitchen and got out another place setting and worked on completing their meal. James called him ahead of time, but they both decided the surprise would be worth it. He smiled as he finished up the meal and called them to the table.

Mike reached over to shake James's hand as they entered the kitchen. "Welcome home, son. I'm so glad you could make it."

"The weather was terrible, but once I got going, I wasn't going to stop. The car is full of my personal stuff, and after the holiday, I'll go back and arrange to close up my apartment. Mom, do you think you have room for me here?"

"Don't be silly. Instead of taking your old room back, you can take the suite that your Dad and I used to use, or the one down here that is opposite of Mike's. Lord knows I have more room than I need. We were always hoping for a passel of grandkids, you know."

"It's not too late. Maybe I'll find the perfect girl yet."

They had a wonderful meal, and Mike felt that Sarah would have been proud of him. He got to know James better over their meal and knew they would become good friends. He continued to watch Edna glow in her son's company, and having him home was the best thing that had happened to her in a couple of years. Mike shooed them off and promised to clean up the mess he had made in the kitchen.

The long weekend flew by, and James left Sunday afternoon for his apartment. He promised to be back in a week. After looking at all of the rooms in the house, he decided to move in on the ground floor. Mike and James moved some furniture around and put some in storage so James could put his own furniture in place. Edna fussed the whole time about James hurting himself, and Mike gave her a hard time because she wasn't worried about his old bones.

True to his word, a small U-Haul showed up a week later, and Mike and James worked on placing the furniture like James wanted it. They had to kick Edna out of the room several times because she kept getting in the way. James finally told her that if she didn't stop bossing him around, he was going to get his own apartment. She stalked away in a huff and went back to the office. The men chuckled, but managed to get everything set like James wanted. There were several boxes they put in a storage room, but James said the rooms looked similar to his apartment and was pleased with the outcome. Mike held his back and was glad James hadn't picked out rooms on the second floor.

The Monday after James moved in, Edna and Janda were hard at work when James walked into the office. "This must be the fierce secretary I keep hearing about."

Janda looked startled, as she didn't know anyone else was in the house. Edna smiled. "Janda, my son Xavier James. James, this is my very efficient secretary, Janda."

Janda stood up and put out her hand. "It's so nice to meet you. I didn't realize there was anyone else here. Your mother kept that a secret from me."

James laughed. "I've heard so much about you and how you staved off the enemy several times while my mom was gone. She should have warned you of my pending arrival. That was mean, Mom." Edna just grinned. Janda looked embarrassed and surprised at the same time. "And Mike helped, you know, so you can be mad at him, too." James continued to watch her, and Janda began to become uncomfortable and sat down. "I'll be around a lot now, so we will have to get to know each other better."

Janda just nodded her head and tried to concentrate on her computer screen but couldn't help look at the tall, handsome man in front of her. Edna smiled at the exchange and saw the look on James' face. She was encouraged by his interest and thought maybe she would get that passel of grandkids yet. James excused himself and said he'd go find Mike and work out in the exercise room. Edna watched Janda watch James walk out of the room.

"He moved home over the holidays," Edna said.

Janda jumped when Edna spoke. She had been watching James intently. "He did? That's nice. So we will be seeing a lot of him then?"

"Yes. A lot."

Janda smiled. "Nice."

They both went back to work, and both were grinning ear to ear, only for different reasons. James spent the next few weeks working with his mother on learning the business. They agreed that if he wanted to take over, he could. Or if he chose not to, then they would sell. Mike helped them fit another desk close by Edna's so they could work side by side. Janda helped answer several questions, and before Christmas, James was sitting by Janda's desk more than his mother's. In fact, Edna was finding more and more reasons to not even go into the office.

Christmas arrived, and Martha and Sarah spent several days decorating the house. James and Mike located a small tree in the grove out back that would have needed to be cut down due to space. The poor thing was being crowded out. They brought it in the house for everyone to decorate. James found the tree when he was the groundskeeper and knew it would be perfect for Christmas. They invited Janda to help them decorate it, and they all had a wonderful time. Then they had hot cider afterward in front of the fireplace.

The storms hit just before Christmas and Janda was not going to be able to go home. Edna invited her to join them, and she was happy to accept. James became very attentive, and she felt an immediate attraction to him from the day they met. They all agreed to get one gift for each other and exchange it on Christmas Day after the meal. Everyone shopped and wrapped their gifts secretly and put them under the tree.

Sarah trusted Mike to get a meal together once again, since he managed not to burn Thanksgiving dinner. She left her lengthy instructions, and he was beginning to enjoy cooking the large meals. At least he didn't have to make all the side dishes, since Sarah already had them fixed. The group ate until they couldn't manage another bite, then decided to move into the sitting room where the tree was proudly decorated and the fireplace was set and waiting for them to light.

James finally couldn't wait any longer and decided he would go first giving out his presents. When Janda opened hers, it was a card that invited her out for an evening of entertainment which included dinner and a show. Embarrassed but delighted, she agreed to go. James beamed.

Janda handed out her presents, and she gave James a gift card at the local men's shop. He looked puzzled. "If you are going to take over for your mother, you need a suit and tie."

Edna roared with laughter and had to agree that the clothes he had been wearing every day were pretty threadbare. "You could at least pick up some new jeans and shirts. You aren't undercover any longer."

James hadn't even thought about the clothes he was wearing. He hadn't bought anything for years, and things were becoming a little ratty. Embarrassed, he agreed with their assessment and promised to take care of it after the first of the year.

Edna handed her presents out, and her envelope to James had a formal letter designating him as a partner in

Chessmore Industries and would become the official CEO in January at the next board meeting. She arranged with Peggy Whethers to announce it at the meeting, and Janda already had it on the agenda. James felt honored that his mother thought he was ready to take over. She didn't tell him that Janda would be able to lead him from here on out. After all, she ran the company very well previously.

Then Edna gave Mike a key to a new Cadillac with the instructions that he had to chauffer her around in it.

"Just don't make me wear the goofy cap," he said. Mike finally handed out his gifts and saved the one to Edna for last. When she finally got to open hers, he said, "Wait. Let me tell you something first." Edna paused in her unwrapping. "I just want to thank you for hiring me and accepting that I'm a lousy guard dog. I have enjoyed working for you all these months, although we never did get to that job description, and I'm pretty sure I haven't received a paycheck in months." Everyone laughed.

"You have taught me how to slow down and enjoy the roses— literally. That garden is magnificent. I have handed off all my security details to Jordan and am no longer employed by anyone else. I still own part of the security alarm company, but I'm basically a silent partner. I am officially retired as of today, but I have a new project I wanted to start on, with your help. You can open the present now but only if you open the envelope first."

Edna looked around, and James shrugged his shoulders. She opened up the envelope first, and there was a coupon for new rose bushes at the local greenhouse. She laughed and agreed that it was the perfect gift. She finished tearing into the wrapping paper and opened up a box which had another box in it. She opened it up and found a jeweler's box. She pulled it out and started to open it.

Mike knelt in front of her as she opened it. "Will you marry me, Edna?"

Edna gasped. She looked at the sparkling ring and then at Mike. She was shocked and kept looking back and forth at the ring and then Mike. James finally spoke up.

"Good gravy, Mother. Say yes."

Edna looked Mike in the eyes, took the ring and put it on her finger, looked back at Mike, and said, "Yes."

Mike grabbed her out of her chair and swung her around, almost knocking the tree over. He put her down, held her close, and said, "I've wanted to do this for a long time."

He took her face in his hands and kissed her long and lovingly. James and Janda clapped and whistled. Edna was embarrassed, but the kiss had tingled clear to her toes.

Looking up at Mike, she said, "I had no idea you felt this way, and do you know what? I didn't know I felt this way either." They both laughed, and Mike kissed her again.

James took Janda to the other room and left the two love birds alone. He took Janda into his arms and said, "I think I might have learned something else from my mother."

"What's that?"

"Kissing is pretty cool stuff."

With that, he kissed Janda soundly on the lips.

Made in United States
Troutdale, OR
12/22/2023

15738885R10141